OTHER BOOKS

The Four
Reverse Harem Urban Fantasy
Legacy
Bound
Hunted
Guardians
Chaos
Descent
Reckoning

The Soul Ties series
New Adult Paranormal Romance/Urban Fantasy
Fated Souls: A Prequel Novella
Soul Ties
Torn Souls
Shattered Souls

Touched By The Dark
Paranormal romance/Urban fantasy

THE FOUR HORSEMEN: GUARDIANS

L J SWALLOW

Copyright © 2017 by LJ Swallow

Editing by Hot Tree Editing

Cover Designed by Andreea Vraciu

All rights reserved.

No part of this book may be reproduced in any form or by any electronic or mechanical means, including information storage and retrieval systems, without written permission from the author, except for the use of brief quotations in a book review.

1

Joss

Vee bolts through the open door, and I follow, but I'm knocked back as her pain and fear project, and the energy created pulses into the hall. I lose my footing and steady myself on the table as if someone pushed me to one side with brute force.

Xander looks between me and the doorway, the photograph of Casey in his hand. "Don't leave Vee outside in the rain. See if she's okay."

I can't move. Vee's energy projects again, and I suck in a breath unsure I can deal with the dizzying intensity.

"Joss?" asks Xander.

I shake my head unable to speak. Xander drops the image on the table and strides out the door, into the rain, while I attempt to persuade my weak legs that I have the strength to follow. Before I move, Xander reappears with

Vee in his arms, her face buried into his chest as he cradles her against him. The energy in the room created by her reaction grows as he sets Vee on the sofa. She sinks back and stares into the space around not registering us.

Vee's wet hair hangs in a sheet around her face, where tears mingle with the water, clothes glued to her body by the rain.

Xander swears and runs both hands across his damp hair, before grabbing the woollen throw rug from the sofa arm and holding it out to her. "Vee. Dry yourself."

She doesn't move. This girl barely exists in the room, but her shock and fear fill the air around. Can Xander sense how bad this is?

"Help her," says Xander and gestures at Vee. "Do your thing."

I half laugh. "'My thing?' I'm struggling here, Xan. Vee's feelings are intense, and I don't know what will happen to me if I touch her."

"Just help her," he repeats. "I'll salvage what I can from this mess, and we can leave. We need to go. Now."

Xander turns away and rips image after image from the wall. He turns to the smouldering files in the waste bins and yanks the half-singed papers out, swearing as flames hits his fingers.

I drag a palm down my face. What if I can't fix her? "Vee," I whisper as I sit beside her. She's immobile, and I dry her face with my sleeve. "Come here."

Placing my arms around Vee does nothing. She's stiff, unyielding, but this is worse than the night she discovered who she was, freaked out, and attacked me.

This Vee doesn't fight.

The anguish continues to flood into me, and I steel myself against the effect this could have. As the powerful emotions keep coming, I'm pushed to my limit. There's too much, too fast, and I can't absorb this all. I can't fix her.

"Vee," I repeat and stroke hair from her face, as I attempt to rouse her. But she's catatonic.

Xander continues shoving everything he can find into a plastic shopping bag, avoiding looking at us. "Is she okay?" he asks, not turning around.

"Sure, Xander. She's fucking brilliant."

Absorbing people's negative emotions always works. I *always* manage to convert them into energy that strengthens me.

This time, I'm too overwhelmed and weakened by Vee's.

"Help Vee," I growl at Xander. "I can only try to ground her. Maybe you can break through to her. You and Vee are closer to each other than we are."

Xander turns to me. "What? No. You are. She likes you."

"Seriously, Xander? You had sex with Vee! That makes you bloody closer to her than me."

He opens his mouth to protest, but the words are useless. I know damn well what happened.

"Xander!" I repeat and point at the bag he grips in his hand. "She needs us. Put that shit down and let's get out of here."

"What if they're around? If whoever did this comes back?"

"I think they're long gone." I glance at the blood staining the rough beige carpet in the room's corner. "Both of them."

"I think Seth did this," says Xander. "Not somebody else."

I shake my head, as if shaking away his words. "Seth? No. I don't think he's the type to murder, then drag bodies around the countryside in his car."

"You trust him too much, Joss. We need to find him."

"Obviously, but we need to help Vee first, for fuck's sake!"

I gently lay her tensed figure back against the sofa and stand. I can't hold anymore; every second with her drains me. "I need a few minutes."

Leaving a speechless Xander, I stride out of the hall into the relentless rain, and the sheer amount of energy absorbed from Vee shakes through my body and switches to anger. I swear and smash my fist against the rough brick wall, and rest my head against it ignoring the pain from my grazed knuckles. My lungs hurt as harsh breaths rasp in and out, and I will myself not to lose control Xander-style.

I don't register the rain pouring onto me until enough overwhelming energy drains away and I can rationally face the situation again. Breathing more calmly, I walk back into the hall, filled with the stench of burnt paper, to find Xander beside Vee, holding her hand and staring up in lost confusion.

"What's happening?" he asks. "Why is she like this?"

I rub an arm across my damp hair. "Because we keep putting her into situations she can't deal with. Right from day one, you've expected Vee to cope with too much. She can't just flick from human to the Fifth like that." I click my fingers.

"Why not? It's what she was created for."

"You're such a cold-hearted bastard sometimes," I snap at him. "Look at her. Can't you see she's suffering?"

Xander stands and backs away from the sofa. "I can't deal with this." He grabs the nearby bag filled with his evidence and heads to the doorway. "Is the car unlocked? I'll drive."

If only Xander could allow himself to acknowledge she's more human than he thinks. However hard he tries to hide it, Xander's fear for Vee matches mine, and not only because

Truth, his secret weapon, is malfunctioning. He cares as deeply and that's messing with his reality.

But he doesn't sense what I do. Her reaction to the girl's death this morning proves something I suspected. Vee can't disconnect from the person she was before we found her. She won't reach full strength until she loses more of her human side.

Logan's words worry me.

What will happen if Vee loses her humanity too?

XANDER

The rain splatters against the windscreen as I focus on driving, and on pushing away my thoughts, but the silence inside the car screws with my concentration. I can't allow myself to connect to Vee's distress, because worrying about her interferes with the ability to focus on my role.

Which confuses the fuck out of me, because my duty to care for Vee is one huge part of that role.

The truth launches at me and I can't stop the words forming in my mind.

I'm scared because I don't know how to help Vee.

Yesterday, I lost hold of the control I need to grip onto, and when the physical need unshackled, so did the desire for an emotional bond. I'd convinced myself that Vee connecting with each of us equally meant I could keep my heart and soul guarded. I could avoid giving my true self to Vee because I was just one of four. But now I know the truth

—I can never deny how I feel about Vee, to myself or her. None of us can.

A powerful need for Vee triggered the first time we touched at Portia's and knocked everything sideways. The instant effect this stranger had on me changed up everything. In the moment, I saw a strength she could have over us all, and I told myself not to weaken and give in to my need for her. Now we've crossed that line, I can't step back. I wanted her out of my system, but now I crave Vee more than ever. After last night, the obsession intensified and nothing is satisfied.

I never expected Vee's strength or for her to step up to me. I never expected her to be my equal. Seeing part of myself in Vee is the problem. I can't cope with the idea she can be lost and hurt in this painful way—because that means I can be too.

I park the car outside the farmhouse and glance in the rear-view mirror. Joss has his arms wrapped around Vee, and she's slumped asleep on his shoulder, her arm across his chest. Relief pushes in that Joss managed to keep her calm. Maybe he can fix her too.

As expected, Heath and Ewan freak the hell out when Joss carries Vee upstairs to a bedroom. I hover around outside as Joss fusses over her, gentle and intuitive in a way I never can be.

"Someone needs to sit with her," he says. "Xander, you fill the others in on what happened back at the hall, and I'll stay here."

We crowd at the bedroom door, like nervous visitors at a hospital patient's bed. He's right. We need to shift into our roles, rather than be paralysed by the situation.

"Is she okay, Joss?" asks Heath, and he heads over to sit on the bed. Worry lines his face, as he looks down at Vee.

Vee, the girl I know he loves as much as we all do but has an easier time showing her.

"Vee isn't hurt," I say, as much to myself, but it comes across as a Xander annoyance.

"Sure, Xander," mutters Joss. He places a hand on her forehead and looks down.

"Is she okay?" Ewan asks.

"I think so. I'm not a freaking nurse though, am I?"

I chew my lip. "She needs out of those clothes."

Joss glances at me, and the others do the same. "She'll lose her shit if she wakes and we're stripping her when she's barely conscious."

He's probably right. No, I *know* he's right. "C'mon she asks us to treat her the same as we would each other. I've had the misfortune of stripping you guys in the past when necessary."

Ewan voices the obvious answer. "Yeah, but Xander, she's still a chick."

"We don't need to take *all* her clothes off. Look at her! She's shivering."

"Oh, for fuck's sake, Xander's right." Heath places a hand on Vee's arm. "Vee. It's Heath. I'm going to take your wet clothes off, is that okay?"

Vee sighs and mumbles, "I'm cold."

"Yeah. Look, I'll just take your jeans off. Is that okay? Then you can climb into bed."

"Sure." She wriggles but can't remove her trousers without Heath's help. "I'm tired."

Heath tugs them down, revealing her naked legs. I turn away, remembering them wrapped around me last night. Wrong on so many levels. *This* is why everything is fucked up.

"Ewan. Let me run through the shit that's happened

since yesterday afternoon." I turn my head back to the guys by the bed. "Joss. Maybe leave Heath with Vee; I doubt she'll be happy about us standing around and staring at her half-naked."

Joss grins. "Good point. Who do you think she'd hit the hardest?"

"I wonder what would happen if she did lose her shit with one of us." Ewan nods at Vee. "Do you reckon she could take us down?"

"I bet she'd win," replies Joss. "What do you think, Xander?"

I clench my teeth. "Let's leave her alone."

As I walk out of the room with Ewan, I hear Heath. "Is that a bruise on Vee's shoulder? What the hell happened?"

Joss and I glance at each other, and I don't miss his amused smile. I arch an eyebrow in warning, and Joss doesn't reply—to me, or to Heath.

Yeah, but she won.

2

Vee

I don't remember coming home.

I only remember my mind blanking and shutting down, leaving me in a darkness I retreated into and hid.

Why am I not stronger than this? I'm the Fifth.

I know the answer. I'm weak because I'm human. I need to leave the old Vee and her reactions to my new world behind. But how?

The familiar scent of the house and the four guys around rouses me. Relief rushes in when I open my eyes; thank God, I'm away from the awful place filled with blood and fear.

Heath's concerned face comes into focus in front of me. I had a hazy dream about him undressing me.

I *am* half-naked. Not a dream.

What happened to me? Why do I have memory gaps?

"Shit, I didn't die did I?" I croak out.

He chuckles. "No, but I undressed you. We thought you'd catch your death if you stayed in those wet clothes."

I reach out and touch his face. "I thought I already caught Death?"

He returns a wry smile. "Glad you've kept your sense of humour. I hope it's okay I did? I asked first."

The worry on his face amuses me. "It's not the first time you've undressed me, Heath. Besides, I'd rather be warm than stuck in wet clothes."

His mouth tips into a smile. "Okay. Good."

He shifts around so he's beside me on the bed, and I snuggle into his chest. He places an arm around me; Heath smells of the comfort he's always ready to offer me. I feel strongly about all the guys, but as Heath and I spend more time together physically, we build a closer physical bond. Heath's tenderness contrasts strongly with what happened with Xander last night.

My cheeks heat at the memory.

I need to talk to Xander about the situation.

"How long have I slept?"

"Just a few hours. Joss and Xander brought you home, and then Xander went straight out to check on Seth's house. Xander's confused and not in a great mood." Heath rests his head on mine. "He explained everything that happened, what you saw. That's fucked up."

"You don't need to tell me that," I say in a hoarse voice.

Heath hugs me tighter. "I feel pretty shit that I didn't stop the pair snatching you from outside the warehouse."

"All good. I can look after myself." I squeeze his fingers. But can I? My breakdown has thrown serious doubt over my ability. What must they think of me? "Besides, we found Seth. Well, he found me."

"And now we've lost him again," says Heath. "He wasn't around."

"What happens next?" I ask.

"We find Seth. We find who's behind the deaths, and we get on top of this. We always win in the end." Heath's firm voice and strong confidence reassures me—a little. His tone changes, and he pushes my face up, fingers beneath my chin. "How are you, Vee?"

The deep concern in his green eyes swells my heart. "I'm okay, Heath."

"I'm glad you can't lie." He runs his finger across my cheek. "I know this shit is tough for you, but I promise we'll do everything we can to stop anybody else dying."

"But can you?"

"Sometimes we take a while to get to the bottom of things, but we always do." He places a soft kiss on my lips. "We've got this. But I'm worried about you," he continues and strokes my hand. "Xander tried to hide how he felt when they brought you home, but I know him. He was totally freaked out."

I press myself into the warmth and safety of Heath's arms. "I don't know what happened. I think everything became too much."

Heath's next words are muffled by his lips in my hair, but strike at the heart of my fears. "I'm worried you're more human than we realised."

"I lived as one for years, involved in everyday life without knowing who I was. I'm more connected to human emotions and the world than you four are, Heath. You always knew. You guys always kept a distance."

"I guess." He shifts away and rests his head against the wall.

"What? You want to say something. Go on."

"Maybe you should stop trying to hold onto that human side as tightly. I think it's clouding your judgement over Seth too."

I tense at his name. "And how do I let go of my human?"

"By making your relationship with us all more complete."

"I already have," I protest. "I've given everything to my relationship with each of you."

Heath screws his face up. "Yes, but only with two of us."

"Two of you?" His expression answers my question. "Oh. Are you suggesting I need to have sex with you all?"

Heath falls silent. His words surprise me because I swore he wanted the human Vee to remind him he could be human too.

"I don't know, Vee. We're not sure what it takes to make you wholly like us, but what happened when we connected —that must mean something. I feel more bonded to you now. Not physically, but deeper inside myself. Does that make sense? Do you feel that deeper bond with Ewan too?"

"Ewan?" Oh. He thinks I had sex with Ewan? He doesn't know about Xander and me?

"No?" he asks.

I take Heath's hand and squeeze. "I'm tired. I've had a shit few days. Can we talk about something else?"

Heath places his thumb beneath my chin and pushes my face upwards so his lips meet mine. We kiss in a way becoming familiar, Heath's gentleness and understanding pouring from his lips and soothing me.

The door clicks closed and I turn my head. Joss stands in the doorway with a mug in his hand, and an expression I rarely see. This isn't jovial Joss, and I sense worry in his aura.

"Don't tell me, you brought a cup of tea to fix me," I say.

My words prompt the smile he's missing.

"Is Xander back?" asks Heath.

"Not yet. He called to say there's no sign of anybody at Seth's. They didn't find many personal documents. A few bills mostly addressed to Casey. No computers either. They did find Nova Pharm payslips, so at least we know they both definitely worked there. He's heading back, and we can decide what to do next."

Joss sits on the opposite side of the bed to Heath and strokes my hair. Joss did this before, when the reaction to the scene in the hall poured out as the rain poured on my head. If Joss hadn't taken some of my anguish into himself, the screaming inside my mind would've filled the hall. His ability to absorb my extreme reactions and emotions pulled me away from the Vee who experiences them too harshly.

He can starve others of emotions; can he starve mine?

I prop myself up in bed and take the mug, cradling the welcome warmth in my hands. Both guys shuffle either side on the bed next to me, and the protectiveness I normally hate shrouds me. Where we touch, I sense their affection, which wipes away the remains of this morning's horrors.

Are they as aware as I am that I'm almost naked beneath this blanket?

It's a bloody good thing we didn't encounter a situation where I used my powers this morning. If my usual response had been triggered, the stirring arousal and suggestive thoughts drifting into my mind wouldn't stay contained.

I glance at Joss, and the smile he fights tells me he's aware what I'm thinking, even if Heath isn't.

Instead, I hold onto the other emotion running through my mind right now

Anger at my weakness.

Heath's right. The old, human Vee needs to go.

The files with burnt corners rest on the table, alongside singed papers and the photos Xander collected from the wall. The guys are as quiet as the day we found the body at the house. Are they staying calm for me? Treading around my feelings because I suffered? I don't want to see the photographs. I hardly knew Casey, but thanks to the images, my two worlds finally collided and my mind exploded.

Xander explains to me that he ran through yesterday's and this morning's events with Heath and Ewan while I rested. I nod, annoyed with how dismissive he is. Xander obviously hasn't told them everything.

How far are they with figuring out the information in front of them? Avoiding looking at the images, I pick up a readable sheet.

"We have to consider why only one of the pair is in these photos," says Xander in a low voice as he taps one. "We don't know whether Seth was attacked or walked away."

Heath's eyes widen as Xander decides not to mince words.

"You think Seth did this, don't you?" I ask. "That he killed all those people?"

"We have to consider it's a possibility," says Joss quietly. "We can't rule anything out."

I don't know Seth, but I bristle at their instant conclusion. "I think Seth will get in touch."

Heath gestures at the folders. "Seth owned all the files, and knows what all this is about. He holds the key to something, whether it's leading us to murders or explaining what he's been doing."

"That's the problem," says Xander. "He's a mystery, and we don't know his motives."

"I expect his current motive is to stay alive," I reply.

Ewan looks at me. "I don't understand what the delay is. Vee's correct, we find the guy. He said he would come back for Vee. One way or another, he will."

"If someone's playing games with us, Seth will appear eventually," says Joss.

Alive or dead?

Xander takes another image and studies it. "Joss told you we drew a blank at Seth and Casey's house. I want to head back to the hall next. We didn't have enough time to look over the place earlier."

I don't miss the undertone. *Because Vee freaked out and had to be taken home.*

"Do you really think Seth will return to where his friend was murdered? I don't. He thought you were responsible for the deaths. I imagine he'll hide from anywhere you might find him."

"Okay, if it wasn't him, Seth must've seen who attacked him and Casey. He knows we're not the people who murdered his friends."

"So we need to help Seth when we do find him," I protest.

Silence.

Have they made their minds up about Seth already?

"Whether he's involved with Casey's death, or is about to become the next victim, we need to find him. The longer we wait, the more likely we never will."

"Which is exactly what I'm suggesting, Vee," growls Xander. "Let me plan where to go. We have done this kind of thing before. I know what I'm doing."

I look to Ewan. "CCTV footage from near the hall?"

He shakes his head. "Someone's erased or hidden it."

"Of course," I mutter.

Xander sweeps the papers into a file. "I'll take Heath and we'll check out the hall, maybe hang around and see if anybody appears."

"I want to go too," I announce.

Xander closes his eyes and inhales sharply. "I don't think that's a good idea after what happened earlier, is it?"

I squeeze my hands together beneath the table. "That's the reason I need to go back."

"What if you freak out again?"

The green eyes that looked into mine with darkened passion last night are filled with doubt. Is he worried about me, or his investigation?

"I won't. Besides, if we do find Seth I'd like to be there."

"Heath?" Xander asks.

Heath blows air into his cheeks. "I think if Vee wants to go, she should. The more exposure she has to this shit, the sooner she'll assimilate."

Assimilate.

I chew my lip and wait for Xander's response. He's outvoted.

3

Vee

By the time we arrive at the town where Casey and Seth were based, the night and cold have set in. I suggested we wait until the morning, but Xander's eager to check the place out as soon as possible. We left Ewan to work through the information we gathered earlier today, and Joss stayed with him. Determined to prove my freak-out performance earlier was a blip, I pushed to come here.

Now I'm unsure. The hall no longer looks like a nondescript council building to me, but a horrific crime scene I don't want to approach.

The car park is empty and the place untouched. I expected police tape—something—but there's no evidence this has become a crime scene.

"Didn't you contact the police about what you found?" I ask.

Xander opens the car door to climb out. "We don't involve ourselves in police investigations."

"You could contact them anonymously?" I suggest as I step into the gloomy November evening.

Heath rests his arms on the car roof as he looks across at me. "The demon Order are everywhere, and that includes the police. We had to search past a false report to find John's death, remember? Someone hid that. We don't want anyone else to know until we've made our own investigation."

"Right." I stare out at the street and away from the hall. Rain trickles onto my hood, and onto the people passing in their humdrum lives. "This hall is in the middle of a town. It's a public facility and not a derelict building. If Casey and Seth hired it, how long for? When do they need to return the keys? Someone will find this soon."

"And we'll be long gone," replies Xander. "Don't stress."

Don't stress? Is he serious?

"Then let's not hang around," I reply. "I'm not comfortable here."

I splash through a puddle as I walk away from the guys and the car. I have a point to prove; I can go back in there and cope this time.

Xander hurries to catch up and Heath walks along side, the pair flanking me. The closer I get, the harder the human Vee attempts to push her emotions through.

I can do this.

I'm strong.

The door is closed but not locked, and Xander examines the door, close to the base. "Nobody's been back here."

"How do you know?" I ask.

He points. "I taped aluminium wire to the door, which breaks easily. It's intact." He pulls at the door and the wire snaps. "So Seth hasn't been back, unless he somehow has the exact same wire as me and attached it."

"Doubtful." Heath looks at me. "Okay?"

"Stop fussing," I say through gritted teeth and stride inside after Xander.

I spent the journey here re-imagining everything I witnessed in preparation for what I might see next. Little has changed in the scene greeting me—the same upturned furniture and message on the wall; the burnt-paper smell still lingers. Xander and Heath set about rummaging through everything. Heath tips a waste bin filled with burnt papers onto the table, but there's little salvageable in the ash. Xander crouches on the floor close to the blood and message, and I search beneath the sofa and in the small kitchen area.

Nothing.

I perch on the sofa and watch Xander who stands in the middle of the room pulling on his bottom lip. The frustration on his face grows, and a glance at Heath shows he's not much happier.

"I told you we found everything already," says Heath.

"Yeah, I just needed to know whether he came back, or if anybody had been here since we left."

"I told you, I doubt he will." I pick at the rug across the sofa. "What do we do now?"

"I want to watch the place," Xander replies. "See if anybody is waiting until dark. Maybe we can check out some other places in town."

"Like where? The pub?" I say sarcastically.

I groan when the guys glance at each other and nod. "Don't forget you're driving, Heath."

"I'm bloody hungry too. Aren't you?" he replies.

"Yeah, let's go."

As Xander strides from the hall, Heath hangs back and says in a low voice. "At least we can regroup and Xander can take some time to mull things over. The longer we go with finding nothing, the more determined he'll be to keep going."

And the worse his temper will get.

Gold lettering on a sign above the opposite building reads "The Lions Inn," and I follow the boys through the green door into the pub. Tables and chairs are crammed into the small space between the doorway and bar; three men at the table closest to us don't register our arrival, eyes fixed on the TV screen above the short bar. The smell of stale beer accompanies my walk across the dirty carpet to a small round table surrounded by low stools. Xander's smile grows when he discovers it's positioned in a small window facing out onto the street. Heavy burgundy curtains obscure part of the view, but the car park and old hall are visible.

The pub is half-full, and judging by their careful scrutiny, most customers are locals. The town doesn't have any features to attract tourists, another commuter settlement that absorbed the original settlement. A few here look like the original residents too; elderly men play dominos at a table close to ours.

Xander orders food, and I watch as the young barmaid flirts with him. He switches on his brighter persona, all smiles and well-rehearsed smoulder, which causes a twinge in my chest. I'm not upset he's flirting, I never expected that behaviour to stop, but he's being *nice*. Me, the girl he had sex with yesterday, enjoys the sullen

Xander, and this one is graced with the man who has girls eating out of his hand.

I have to fight him for everything.

"You okay?" asks Heath and laces his fingers through mine. "Was it too much for you to come back here?"

"No. I'm tired. Life's non-stop."

Heath pulls me to him in a hug and kisses the top of my head.

"Yeah. You'll get used to it."

I'm glad he can't see my expression anymore because I'm not feeling great right now.

Xander returns with two pint glasses and an orange juice between his hands. He sets them on the table and pulls out the opposite stool.

"What?" he asks "Why are you looking at me like that?"

"Were you flirting with her or getting information?"

Xander picks up his glass and drinks slowly, watching me from over the edge. His expression annoys me because I can't read his eyes or what he's thinking.

"Information," he says and places his glass down. "Ever considered we look the way we do for a reason? It's sure as hell easier to talk people around when you can charm them."

"And you're such a charmer, Xan," says Heath with a laugh.

"Yeah, I guess the Four Middle-aged, Overweight Horsemen of the Apocalypse wouldn't have the same success with charming the female population into helping them," I reply. "Fortunate."

Xander breaks into a smile. "Hence your alluring self."

"Huh?"

"Because you have a piece of each of us inside you of course you're attractive too."

"This is a bizarre conversation, Xander," replies Heath. "Have you been brooding over who we all are, again?"

"I don't brood, that's your job, emo guy."

"I should do it your way, huh? Hold everything in until I explode?"

"He sure does explode," I reply, and fix my eyes on Xander.

Xander runs his tongue along his teeth. I'm pissed off he hasn't spoken to me about what happened in the hotel. Not just the room-shattering sex but the affection afterwards. He's withdrawn again. Has he returned to distrusting me?

But why compare him to the open and affectionate guy holding my hand? Our relationship is nothing like mine with Xander. Or any of the others. Isn't that what I like? That they are all different—that we complement each other in different ways?

"So what did you question her about?" I ask.

"Whether anybody who looks like Seth or Casey have visited. No, apparently. 'Other people don't come here' were her words."

Heath smirks and sips his beer. "Beware of the locals."

Following Xander's words, the other patrons' scrutiny unnerves me further. Bloody ridiculous I'm worried about what these people think after my recent experiences.

The guys fill themselves with the usual junk: pies, chips, beer. My appetite isn't great, and I'm touched by their fussing when I choose pumpkin soup.

"I hope we don't need to chase anyone," I say as Heath pushes his plate to one side. "You'll get a stitch."

He shakes his head with an amused smile. "I'm sure I'll be fine."

Xander's attention is drawn to the window through most of the meal, and he misses my comment to Heath. I look over as Xander straightens again and cranes his neck, as a guy walks by. The man keeps walking and doesn't cross over to the hall; Xander's shoulders slump again.

"If you're done here, maybe we can switch our focus elsewhere?" I suggest. "It's late, we've had a hell of a day, and maybe things will be clearer tomorrow? Ewan could have more info."

Xander taps the beer mat on the table. "I want to stay. And I don't mean for more beer."

"We haven't seen anyone go inside," I reply.

"Another half an hour?" suggests Heath. "Compromise."

"Fine." Xander places his elbows on the table, hands beneath his chin as he switches his attention back to the window.

4

VEE

Xander's smug triumph joins his words. "Look! Told you!"

Heath shifts his stool closer to Xander, and I lean over to join them in looking through the grimy window. A tall figure in a short, dark jacket climbs from a motorcycle in the car park outside the hall. He pulls off his helmet and leaves it on the bike before hunching against the rain and walking towards the hall.

"Score!" Xander's eyes shine as he looks to us. "I told you waiting was the right thing to do."

Draining his beer, Xander stands and grabs his coat. "Let's go."

I hurry after them outside into the drizzle, and we splash across the road to Heath's car. Xander opens the car boot and sorts through the items permanently stashed inside. A long bowie knife gleams in the light cast by a nearby streetlight as he holds it up.

"What if he's human, Xander? You can't kill him," I say.

He hands it to me. "You can be the judge of that."

The knife is heavy in my hand, and I debate whether to give the weapon back. I don't need this.

"Take it, Vee," replies Heath.

Xander pulls out two more. "I don't want to use powers on the one guy, in case he's bait and there's a horde of others waiting to attack. A knife will do."

A thought strikes me as he sheathes and then tucks the knife into his jacket. Did Xander agree I could join them because he thinks we'll need my powers? Is he finally trusting my ability, despite my inability earlier?

"Plan?" Heath asks Xander.

"Stay undercover and watch what he does. If he stays inside the hall, we follow. If he comes back out, we grab him. Whoever the hell it is, they have info."

The grassed area between the car park and hall is muddy, and we squelch through, keeping to the shadows. As we move to the building rear again, Xander holds up a hand to indicate we stop. The door is ajar and the two figures appear, one dragging the other from the building. Light shining from inside casts across the pair, and my heart skips out of rhythm when I see who one is.

The brown-haired guy's wearing glasses, but that's the only Seth-like part of his appearance. Seth's clothes are dishevelled, and he doesn't struggle against the grip the guy has around his neck. The biker guy's face illuminates briefly, impassive and unremarkable, but the strength he has over Seth isn't.

"Shit!" mutters Heath.

"What the hell is Seth doing back here?" growls Xander. "How did we miss him?"

I move to run toward the pair, but Xander grips my arm. "No. Wait."

"What?" I hiss. "Seth could be about to die!"

Heath rubs his forehead with the back of his sleeve. "She's right. Come on."

The man holding Seth drags him into the trees bordering the building. "Go after him!" I urge.

"Check the building," he says to Heath. "I'll deal with the guy and Seth. Vee, hang back and watch Heath."

Xander unsheathes his knife and walks into the shadows, his back to the wall as he creeps beneath the building's eaves in the direction of the trees. Heath takes my hand and squeezes.

"You okay, Vee?"

I look away from his concerned smile. No. I'm not the Vee who was here earlier. I'll prove I'm stronger than her. Seth won't die too.

ANDER

Well this adds a new dimension to the situation.

I only glimpsed his face for a few moments, but I've encountered this guy enough to know who he is. Taron, the mercenary who has the cheek to call himself a supernatural vigilante. Did Heath not recognise him too?

The last time I searched for Vee alone, I encountered Taron. I suspected, and accused, him of looking for Vee too.

He refused to admit this, claiming he was searching for a rogue shifter drawing too much attention to a local pack. His job isn't too far removed from ours, and as he's a vamp against other supes, we allow him to work as long as he keeps his hands and weapons off humans.

If Taron doesn't kill humans, so why is he with Seth?

From my hiding place, I watch and weigh up the situation as Taron holds Seth against a nearby tree trunk, Seth's feet off the ground. I strain to hear their urgent voices and catch Seth's panicked tones. My muscles coil, ready to intervene and judging by what's happened to his friends, this situation doesn't look good for Seth.

Surely Taron can't be responsible for the other human deaths? The victim's injuries and taunting messages aren't his modus operandi, so what the hell is happening here?

Taron drops Seth to his feet, who grips the trunk, pushing himself back as if trying to blend in and escape. As Taron lifts his arm, hand curled into a claw ready to strike, I charge forward and slam into him. Caught by surprise, Taron loses his footing and sinks to the floor, and Seth cries out as Taron's claw-like nails dig into his arm. Seth lands on the ground too, clutching the wound.

Taron's anger shifts to shock as he looks up from the leaf-littered ground to where I stand over him. Strands of black hair escape his ponytail, and his dark eyes glitter in his pale face.

"What are you doing?" I snarl and slam a boot onto Taron's chest. "He's human."

Taron makes an 'oof' sound and grabs my ankle but can't move me. "I was given a job to do."

"To kill him?" I press my boot harder.

Taron coughs a laugh at me. "How's life, Horseman?"

"Safer than yours is right now." I snap my head around to

Seth, whose white face matches that of the vampire right now. "Seth, get back into the hall. Heath and Vee are in there. You'll be safe."

The guy doesn't need asking twice. He scrambles to his feet and bolts around the corner to the doorway, almost losing his footing on damp leaves.

I look down at his assassin, pissed off there's no fear in his passive face. "Who hired you to kill Seth?"

"No idea. My employers don't often reveal their names, do they? I didn't realise he was your mate!"

"Get up!" I demand and remove my foot. The moment Taron's on his feet, I yank him by the shirt so we're nose to nose. "Did you kill the girl?"

"What girl?"

"His friend."

"First time I've met the guy. Don't know anything about him."

This doesn't add up. I push Taron against the tree he held Seth against, itching to end his life with the knife in my jacket, but control the urge. Taron has answers. We find those first—then he dies. This rogue vamp always trod on thin ice, thanks to his activities, and he just fell through.

"How did you know Seth would be here?" I ask.

"The human? He was dumped here an hour ago—I waited for a text telling me to come. I was warned you might be around, but we have an understanding, yeah, Xander?"

I narrow my eyes. Is that why someone chose to recruit Taron? Because he's above suspicion by the Horsemen? "No."

"Hey, I helped you in the past."

I lean in and growl into his face, "Killing a human breaks our treaty, Taron."

"I didn't know he was human until I arrived!"

"But it didn't stop you, did it?" I snarl. "Tell me who hired you."

"Like I said, no fucking clue. Money is in my bank account. I do my job, and I'm set for retirement with that kind of money." Taron's impassive attitude doesn't change, which pisses me off more. Doesn't he realise the shit he's landed himself in?

I drag Taron away from the tree, then spin him around and lock an arm around his throat. "How about I take you inside and see if I can jog your memory."

Taron finally struggles against me as I half drag the reluctant vamp across the ground towards the building. He matches my height, though his slim build is deceptive. Vampires are strong. Me? Stronger. Always. The situation could've ended badly for Seth, but I'm lifted by the hope we could have a real lead.

5

Xander

In the hall, a battered Seth sits on the sofa holding his arm. Poor guy looks like he's been through some shit. Either Taron roughed him up first, or someone else is responsible for his torn clothes and bruised face.

Heath wraps a makeshift tourniquet made from Seth's shirt around his arm, while Vee stands beside them, her knuckles white around the blade held in front of her.

Oh fuck, she'd better not freak out again.

"What the hell?" says Heath. "Taron? What the fuck are you doing here?"

"Nice to see you, man."

I bristle at his smug attitude. Does he really think he's getting out of here alive? I pull an overturned chair upright and shove Taron onto the seat. "Talk."

He ignores me and turns his head to appraise Vee. "This Truth? You found her, then? She's cute."

Vee points the knife in Taron's direction. "Who is he?"

He continues to trace an interested gaze over Vee as Heath answers her. "He's a vamp. Rogue. Works as an assassin but for supes, not humans."

"Are your colleagues involved?" I interrupt. "Should I look outside for them, too?"

"Colleagues?" Taron snorts. "You mean Syv and her deadbeat friend? We're not colleagues."

I don't care what he says, Taron trades information and occasionally clients with Syv and Abel. Syv's activities are less blood-thirsty than Abel and Taron's; she'll kill if asked but her expertise in locating and "rehoming" magical items pays her more. Nobody knows exactly what or who she is, but we've never had issues with her. Abel–another vamp and a straightforward, skilled assassin. He's hit our radar a couple of times, but is aware we watch what he's doing.

"You work together," I reply.

"No, we respect each other's work and sometimes pass on info. No way was I sharing this job with them."

"Why?" asks Heath.

"What can I say? I had an offer too good to turn down that I didn't want them getting a sniff of. Mine's a dangerous job, and the cash I'm being paid for this would set me up for a long time. Twenty year holiday, maybe."

I stare down at him. His hair and clothes are damp from outside, black jacket open across a black shirt. Dark denim covers his legs and his boots could kick someone into next week if needed. The dark brown eyes set in his gaunt face are rimmed by red. He pushes strands of hair from his eyes, his long nails covered in blood. "Paid for by who?"

"I said I have no fucking clue."

"The money magically appeared in your account?" says Heath derisively.

"Half did. The rest arrives once I provide evidence the job's done."

"He's lying," says Vee. "Taron met the person, but doesn't know who he is."

"Who? Demon? Human?" I snap

Taron shrugs, then tips his head towards Vee again. "Do you know how to use the knife, sweetheart? You don't look like you'd be much help to anybody."

Fuck this. I punch Taron in the face, bone cracking on bone, but he just wipes the blood from beneath his nose and laughs at me.

"How many humans have you killed?" I snarl.

"None. This would be the first. I didn't know he was, or I wouldn't have taken the job!"

"But you didn't walk away, Taron." I jab a finger into his chest. "You could've walked away. Stupid move, man."

"Who was it you saw?" interrupts Heath.

Taron rocks the chair back onto two legs. "Human. Maybe? I dunno, hard to tell sometimes. The guy was tall. I think."

"You think?"

The bravado drops from his expression and his brow knits. "I'm not sure, he looked..." He hits the side of his head with a palm as if attempting to push a thought into place. "Tall. Hair was... Dunno." He blinks. "I can't picture him anymore."

"Oh yeah, how fucking convenient." I reward his lack of information with another punch.

Taron's head reels back and the chair almost tips. He rights himself and scowls at me. "Beat the shit out of me if you want, but I don't have any answers."

"Bullshit," I growl.

I rub my knuckles and stand over him. The guy knows who we are, and he'd be stupid to fuck with us, but he's bloody trying. I'm tempted to cover that sneering face in more blood, and if he doesn't talk soon, I'm going to lose my shit.

Taron jerks and his eyes widen, before he takes a huge gasping breath. Huh, I didn't hit him that hard.

"Just talk, Taron, and we might be nicer to you," says Heath.

"Speak for yourself," I mutter.

Taron heaves another breath and squeezes his eyes closed. "Fuck!" His body jerks again and trembling runs through his arms, spreading to his legs. What the hell? He doubles over and attempts to clutch the sides of the chair, and wheezes.

I step back. This isn't a performance for us. "Taron?"

He lifts his head and stares at Seth who returns his terrified look. "Chaos. It's fucking chaos," he rasps out.

"Yeah that's one word to describe the situation," snorts Heath. "You have no idea the shit you're involved in."

Taron continues to choke as if I held my hands around his throat. He shakes his head, eyes bulging as he drags nails at his chest and scratches until blood seeps through the shirt. Taron tugs in desperation and rips at his collar as if the material suffocates him.

Shit. Magic? How much time do we have? "Is anybody else coming here?"

He shakes his head and jabs a finger at Seth as garbled sounds come from his mouth.

"What? Is he in danger? Who wants him dead? Tell us!"

Heath approaches and places a hand on my arm. "I don't think we'll get any more info out of Taron."

I drag both hands though my hair and swear.

Vee steps forward and breaks her silence. "What's that?" She points at his shoulder with her knife.

Taron's torn shirt reveals the edges of a glowing mark on his chest, above the collarbone. I pull his shirt further to one side ignoring his desperate whimpering as he grips at my wrist.

A circular, runed symbol I've never seen before glows white with an intensity to match the light Heath can produce. I've seen runes branded on creatures many times, but scorched or drawn, not this. I'm no expert, but I don't recognise it either. Fae or demon runes have hallmark symbols incorporated, but there's none in this simplistic one.

"Who did that?" I ask, but Heath's right. Seth isn't about to answer any more questions.

The guy's energy ebbs as his eyes well with blood, and when he opens his mouth to speak blood gushes between his lips. I've seen vamps die many times, usually when I slice their heads off, and I give them clean deaths. Instant. If I'd want to torture one, I'd skewer their dark hearts and watch as the creature drowns slowly and painfully in its own blood.

Like this.

But he wasn't injured when we found him, and his self-inflicted scratches didn't do this. What the fuck is happening?

The blood continues to flood from Taron's mouth and pools on the floor. He stares back at me, immobile, the expression telling me he's aware as we are he won't survive.

"Kill him," whispers Heath. "I don't want to watch this."

I waver. He means Vee shouldn't watch this. I've dealt with Taron as an uneasy ally. We don't get along, but until today, I thought we were on the same side. Maybe it's not too late to get info from him.

What the hell is the mark on his shoulder?

Distracted by my thoughts, I don't have a chance to respond when Vee steps between us, holding her knife horizontally. I reel when she shoves the blade hard into Taron's bloodied throat, remembering the day outside, when I showed her the knives and told her she could kill or defend herself. But this isn't self-defence.

Taron's head separates from the neck as if Vee sliced through butter, the way I told her when she was hesitant back then. The blood flow stops, cauterised by the silver in the knife as it does with the species, and she stares down as the head tumbles to the floor. Taron's body slumps and he rolls from the chair.

Holy shit.

His hands begin to shrivel as the decay from death held at bay for years takes hold, and I whip out my phone to photograph the mark that killed him, before his body disintegrates

I wait for Vee to collapse back onto the sofa beside her human friend, but she remains upright, staring down at the scene in front of her. Seth groans and drops his head onto the sofa arm muttering, breathing laboured in panic.

Heath joins in my stunned staring at Vee. Turning away from the body, she drops the knife to the floor and looks to me. The last time we were here, and she witnessed death, Vee's eyes filled with terror.

This time they glitter in anger, and in them, I recognise myself.

"He killed people, now I've killed him," she says in a low voice. "He was going to kill Seth."

I look to the ceiling. Vee helped end his suffering, but

would she have ended his life anyway? Did her need for revenge take over, and she lashed out without thinking?

I don't need to ask myself these questions because I'm acutely aware of the answers.

When War takes hold, thinking switches off.

6

Vee

Seth walks into the farmhouse, hesitant as he looks at the surroundings, holding his hand over the wound. Xander walks ahead and Heath hangs back with us. Is Seth's pale face due to the wound or his nerves around the guys? As he's about to be interrogated by Xander, probably both.

Ewan appears in the doorway and halts for a moment as he sees Seth, welcoming face switching to narrow-eyed suspicion. "So this is the elusive DoomMan, huh? What happened to your friend?"

Ewan strides over and I stand between him and Seth. "He's injured, Ewan. Back down." Ewan's eyes flick over Seth's bloodied jacket. "We found him back at the hall."

Seth rests against the wall, perspiration covering his pallid face. Heath managed to stop the bleeding, but I'm worried by the amount of blood soaking through his shirt.

I place a hand on Seth's in an attempt to comfort.

"Was that his teeth?" asks Ewan.

Seth shakes his head and grimaces. "Nails."

"He needs medical treatment," replies Xander. "But we didn't want to leave him at the hospital. I'm not letting this guy out of my sight again."

"Yeah, I agree we should talk to Seth before he disappears again," says Ewan in a low voice. "I'd like to hear what happened to Casey, and where he's been today."

"Xander's right." Joss nods at Seth. "What if the demons succeed in killing him next time?"

Seth takes a sharp take of breath. "Take me to a hospital. I don't care."

I expected Xander to be the one reluctant to allow Seth into the house, not Ewan. He's never met the guy; he shouldn't form an opinion until we talk.

"Yeah, but we don't let people on the property," says Ewan to the guys. "That was always our rule."

This conversation's pointless. Seth needs help, and the other guys clearly don't want to. "Joss." I take Seth by his uninjured arm. "He needs help with his wounds."

Joss helps me guide Seth into the kitchen where he sits him at the table. I look away as Joss peels away the blood-soaked shirt tourniquet and studies the wound. "That's a hell of a gash."

Seth forces a smile. "Fucking hurts."

"Vampire," I say.

Joss's head jerks up. "Vampire? Is that who's killing people?"

"Xander doesn't think so."

"Yeah, most victim's injuries suggest demon not vampire. Apart from Seth. What happened out there?"

"We killed it," I say. "Xander and Heath can tell the rest."

Seth rests his head on the table, eyes closed and face ashen. What does he think about our vampires conversation, or what happened to him? Does Seth think he's hallucinating in pain?

I locate and drag the first aid box from the cupboard, remembering the day Xander cleaned up my wound. Somehow I can't picture Xander as the one who'll help out today.

Joss digs around in the box and pulls out needles and surgical thread.

Ugh, no.

"I hope you have medical training," says Seth weakly.

"I won't hurt as much the other guys." He places a hand on Seth's arm. "Don't be nervous."

"You have a calming bedside manner," says Seth and coughs a laugh.

Joss chuckles. "You have no idea. Vee, get Seth something strong to drink. I'm sure that'll help."

I cross the kitchen and pour Seth a whiskey before excusing myself. I've a million questions for Seth, as I'm sure the others have too, but I'm not asking them while Joss stitches up his arm.

What happened to him in the last day?

I imagine Seth has a few questions for us too, after what he witnessed.

Xander, Heath, and Ewan sit in the lounge, and as I walk in, Xander indicates I should close the door. Heath and Xander's shirts are stained with blood, and I look down at mine. Blood. I wait for the rush of nausea. Nothing. Good. Progress.

"I've given Ewan a run down on what happened with Taron. Are you okay?" asks Xander.

"Fine."

"You *sure* you're okay, Vee? What you did back there was..." Heath trails off.

I swallow. I have no words either. My rage took over the moment Xander implied the vampire had killed Casey—and attempted to murder Seth. He didn't deserve to live. The anger surges again, still contained and wanting an outlet. *Every evil, horrific creature in this world deserves to die, and I will do everything to stop them. I'll kill a thousand of the bastards and not care.*

Whoa. "Yes. Fine. Seth's not dead and that's what matters."

Ewan chews on his lip as he studies me; I don't like the distance in his eyes. Heath and Xander were quiet on the way home, and the glances they gave made me uncomfortable, as if seeing part of me for the first time. I don't understand why. I've killed before.

This time, instead of resisting the War overcoming me, I held on, determined to prove my strength and ability to deal with the threat. That determination took over, and I helped.

Didn't I?

"I have a question, Heath." Xander crosses his arms. "How did we miss seeing someone dump Seth?"

Heath straightens. "I don't know."

"I asked you to watch while I was at the bar." He gestures between Heath and I. "Were you paying attention?"

"Mostly. Maybe I didn't spend my whole time nose to the window!" he retorts.

"You screwed up. We could've seen who it was."

The tension in the air thickens between the brothers.

"Maybe they took him in from a different side of the building?"

Xander scowls. "I don't care. This was a fuck up."

"There's nothing we can do now, Xander," I say.

"Have you had a chance to ask Seth any questions?" continues Xander.

"Not in his current state. Please leave Joss to stitch him up, Xander. I think when Seth's rested, he'll be up to an interrogation."

Xander screws his face up, and I'm impressed by his self-control when he sits on a nearby armchair instead of launching himself into the kitchen.

"Where's he been, Vee? What happened to him today?" Ewan asks.

"We don't know."

I pick up an emotion from Xander I'm sure he doesn't want to share—uncertainty. For Seth's sake, I hope the frustration resting beneath doesn't take him over. "Seth has a lot of explaining to do if he wants to stay here."

"I'm sure both sides have a lot of questions to ask," I reply.

Heath nods. "He saw us killing a vampire tonight. A vampire sent to kill him. Now we can be certain that whatever happened to his group has a demon connection."

Us killing? Me. I sit on the sofa beside Ewan as the three continue to discuss Taron, and I sigh at yet another connection in the Horsemen's world I have no clue about. Ewan takes in the new information with an enthusiastic relief to match Xander's earlier and heads to his laptop for research.

As the anxiety over Seth ebbs and the anger from my War finally drops, another energy triggers. I should be exhausted after the last thirty-six hours, but I'm invigorated after War took hold and the energy surged inside. I struggle to focus on Xander's words, and staying present, but my power's hunger for something more stirs. I want the release I only achieve through sex with one of the guys.

I don't have the strength to fight that side of myself; I'm aware how the night will end.

In the kitchen, Joss tidies away bloodied gauze and Seth lies with his head on the table, outstretched arm covered in a fresh cream-coloured bandage. Seth's mouth is parted in sleep, head still covered in perspiration, damp hair sticking to his forehead. Bruises mark his cheeks and around his eyes, and there are more on his exposed arms. What happened to Seth? Who did this?

"Did you put him to sleep?" I ask Joss. "Can you do that?"

Joss drops the used bandages and gauze into the waste bin. "Not exactly. Seth passed out, and I encouraged him to stay that way."

"Encouraged?" I ask and Joss raises a brow at me. "I won't ask."

"Are *you* okay?" he asks.

"Me? It annoys me when you all constantly ask. Yes, I am. I know you all think it's strange what I did to Taron but—"

"Not, that, Vee." He flicks on the tap to wash his hands. "You channelled War tonight. We all know what happens when you use your powers."

I close my eyes. "You're sensing it, aren't you?"

"Your raging hormones? Yep."

"Don't worry, I won't jump on you."

"Shame." He throws me a Joss grin and flicks the tap off. "Grab me a beer, will you?"

Seth remains quiet, unmoving against the table, and I stand with Joss by the kitchen counter as we both drink one.

In my time here, I'm acquiring a taste for bottled beer. Maybe that's part of my Horseman "assimilation"?

"What's funny?" asks Joss.

"Oh. Nothing." I drink. "But there's something weird Heath said, and I want to talk to you about it."

"Uh huh. Heath says weird shit a lot. Was he philosophising again?"

"Funny. No. Heath said something about me and my human side. Can I talk to you? I want another opinion."

Joss blows air into his cheeks. "Right. I don't want to discuss things with other ears around." He points at Seth. "Maybe we can talk in the study? Wait there a sec."

Joss leaves the room and I drink my beer, while watching Seth.

Joss returns a few moments later with Xander. "Watch your hostage for a few. Me and Vee have something to talk about."

Xander sits on the edge of the table. "Oh, really? Talk, huh?" He smirks at Joss and refuses to look at me.

"Ha! I wish," says Joss. "I don't think we're past first base yet."

"Shut up," I warn them and point at our captive. "Someone else is here, remember?"

"Yeah, but Vee can't control herself sometimes. Watch it or she'll pin you to the floor." Xander turns his face to me, and I refuse to look away from his challenging stare.

I wait for a Joss joke, but none comes.

Xander breaks our stand off. "Fine. I'll watch your friend. Go *talk*."

Throwing Xander a tight smile, I follow Joss from the kitchen.

7

VEE

I've peeked through the doorway into the study a few times, but never walked in. The room is unofficially Joss's, mostly due to the fact the other guys have no interest in books. Occasionally, Ewan trades the kitchen table for the dark wood desk inside, where his laptop fights for space amongst piled books. Each guy has a spot he's happy to spend time alone, and this is Joss's.

I follow Joss into the room; he draws the heavy burgundy curtains and switches on a shaded lamp beside the desk. He slams a large black book closed and pushes it to one side, then perches on the table edge and stretches out his legs.

Joss is right about my heightened desire. I'm distracted by his biceps tensing as he places his hands behind him on the desk, the hands that have touched me in comfort that could do so much more. Joss's gentleness with Seth, and intuitive nature around me, blooms a warmth in my chest that attracts me to him as much as the man beneath his clothes.

And something inside me whispers, suggesting wicked things I could ask him to do.

Joss rubs long fingers across the mouth I just imagined kissing. "What did Heath say to you? He has a habit of overthinking, especially when tired or stressed. I hope he hasn't upset you again."

"Where do you think you came from, Joss?" I blurt. "Or me?"

He blinks. "I don't know what to believe. I read a lot, as you know, studied the Biblical stories about us—the Four Horsemen I mean. The other guys don't believe any of that is true, but I think Lucifer is connected to us."

"You believe in God and Lucifer?" I ask in surprise.

"Some days." He runs a hand across his hair. "Demon realms exist the other side of the portals. What if one of those places is Hell? Or the big guy stuck back there, who the demons work for, is Lucifer, or equivalent?"

I drop myself into a nearby upholstered chair. "So if you're connected in the way the Bible portrays the Horsemen, do you think you hold this darkness that Logan mentioned I had?"

Joss's mouth parts in realisation. "Is that why you're asking? Are you still concerned about his words?"

"No, about the darkness. It's true, we're killers. I used to think that was wrong, but now... I don't know. Look at me today. Freaked out and sickened by death, but then killing someone. How can I be both?"

"Don't overthink things, Vee," says Joss in a soft voice. "I understand why the fae don't fully trust us when our background is sketchy, and I admit I worry about the dark stories, but not the way Heath and Ewan do."

"They think the darkness will overcome them, don't they?"

Joss holds my look. "They think too much."

"And I can't believe that you don't."

"Well, I could sit around worrying, or I can do what I'm here for. I live day to day." He's not lying, but he's not convincing either of us. "What was it you wanted to know? Besides whether we're really agents of Lucifer?"

"Don't joke like that."

"Sorry."

I dig my nails into my palms. I've rehearsed the conversation, and questioned whether I should ask Joss to do what I'm about to ask, and with the energy running through from killing, I'm pushed closer to asking.

"How I reacted earlier today. When... Casey. I don't think I want to hold onto human Vee anymore. It's too painful. Confusing." I catch worry from Joss's mind before he blanks his emotion. "Do you think I can—and will—lose the human me? I want to be a hundred percent the Fifth."

Joss rubs a palm back and forth across his mouth and disappointment sinks into my stomach at his silence. "But we are partly human, Vee. All of us. Maybe you don't cope as well because you're a—"

"If you're going to say because I'm a girl, stop."

"I wasn't."

I cross my arms. "I don't want to be human anymore, because I never was. The human Verity can't contain Truth; she's too powerful."

"Vee, stop," says Joss in a low voice.

"Can you take away how I feel, Joss? I don't want my old connection to the world and to people anymore. I can't be *this* and experience horror and fear over the death around me." The words tumble from my mouth, the thoughts mulled over and over since my conversation with Heath.

"You'll get used to the death and be able to put the distance there. You managed to tonight, and did before."

"But the human sneaks in and look what happened this morning!"

Joss rubs his brow. "Vee, we all went through accepting this."

"But are we the same? I lived as a human, not the way you did. I don't even know if I *am* created equally to you."

My chair is close to the desk Joss sits on, and he reaches out a hand. I uncross my arms and allow him to take my fingers. The calm sweeps over me as he pulls away part of my distress but barely touches the unease.

"When I discovered I wasn't human that first night, I freaked. As you know." I attempt a smile. "But whatever I am took over within hours, and I coped with the news. Yet, even though I've accepted who I am, there're parts of human Vee left. I thought I wanted to hold onto her, but I realise I can't. There's no room for her with me anymore."

I can't fathom Joss's expression as he studies me in silence. "Yes, there is," he says finally.

I push on. "You can starve people of emotions. Is that permanent? Can you take away mine, so I don't feel intense human emotions?"

His fingers tighten around mine. "No."

No he can't, or no he won't?

"Joss, please." I stand and look down at where he's sitting, and nudge one of his legs, so I can position myself between his thighs. Lacing my fingers around his neck, I hover my mouth above his. His cologne's scent stirs more inside, pushing my memories back to times we've fooled around in bed, but never gone further than maddening kisses and touches. The repressed sexual need for him is pushed higher by a hungry desire for Joss to fix my situation.

I settle my body against his, pushing myself harder against his warm chest as I slide my lips across his stubbled cheek. As the raw energy flowing inside rises further to the surface, I move my mouth onto Joss's and tug on his bottom lip insistently. When he doesn't respond straightaway, I tease him into returning my kiss. Joss slides his hands onto my hips and kisses me gently. I kiss him harder, holding onto his neck and feeling his jawline beneath my fingers.

Happiness hummed through my world the last time I kissed Joss, on our strange date. This time something more intense joins us, and his gentleness switches to urgent. If Joss lets go, he'll do what I'm asking.

They will all do what I ask them to.

I wrench my mouth from his in response to the words entering my head. What the hell was that?

"Are you okay?" He brushes his lips along my cheek and kisses the pulse point on my neck.

I place a hand on his chest to steady myself. "*Will* you help me, Joss?"

There's a soft sadness in his eyes as he strokes my hair. "I'll do anything for you, Vee, but I won't hurt you."

"If you take away how deeply I feel about what happens to humans, you *will* help me." I sneak a hand beneath his shirt and run my nails along the solid muscle beneath. "You'll help all of us. Please."

"No. I won't take away your humanity. You need to hold onto who you are."

Annoyed, I crash my mouth onto his again, and he responds with a harsh kiss. I push him backwards onto the table and climb onto his lap, looking down. Joss looks back, chest moving rapidly. I shift against him, aware how instantly I arouse him and smile.

Dipping my head, I run my tongue along his parted lips. "Okay, if you'll do anything for me, then help with what I need right now."

He cups the back of my head and holds my mouth to his, teasing me with a gentle kiss. No. He needs to let go, not rein himself in. I need to trigger his power the way I do the others. I sit back again and pull my shirt over my head. His gaze immediately switches to my breasts swelling against the black lace bra, while I slowly unbutton his shirt, pushing the material to one side and soaking up the sight. I drag my nails across his smooth skin over the sinewed muscle in his broad shoulders, down his chest towards the solid abs.

Time and time again I've lain in bed with Joss, held against him, feeling his arousal and fighting mine. Why has he never taken the next step? We've never been skin against skin before. Is that how he resisted the desire that winds around us when we're together? I've dreamed about exploring his body, picturing how, and I lean forward to kiss his skin, alternating with nipping. Joss winds his hands into my hair.

"You have no idea how much I fucking want this." His voice is darker than a few moments ago, more ragged. "Or how hard it is to hide from you what I do to you in my dreams."

He doesn't need to tell me, our empath connection broadcasts our desire as the powerful need grows. I look down, my hair touching his face as our eyes meet in understanding.

"Show me what you do in your dreams."

Joss's eyes darken at the words, and he grabs my ass,

holding me to him. Parting my lips with his tongue, he claims my mouth and finally kisses me the way I want.

As Joss absorbs my aching desire, he takes in my raw emotions too. I'm right. He can do this. Joined with him, I could allow him to take too much and starve me of those emotions.

But the love and affection beneath his lust holds him back from letting go and consuming. I deepen my kiss, urging him on. The more of the energised Vee he connects with, the more Joss will loosen his control.

He needs to give in to this.

Joss pulls his head away. "Vee."

"Joss?" I move my head down and place my lips on his chest. I kiss downwards, running my tongue along his smooth skin, inhaling his fresh scent as I taste him. I stop as I reach his abs, then nip gently.

"Are you only doing this so I'll do what you asked?" he asks, voice rough.

I move further down and flick open the button on his jeans. "No. I'm doing this because I want you, too."

"But I know the others lost control around you," he breathes out. "Their powers trigger, I mean. I don't know —" I unzip his fly and run a hand along the erection beneath his briefs. "*Fuck*."

"You don't know if you can control yourself around me? Are you worried you'll absorb too much?"

Starve me of humanity?

"This isn't good, Vee." He swears under his breath as I release his hard cock and curl my fingers around the base.

"This isn't good?" I murmur.

"No. You. Behaving like this. Something's different."

I smile to myself with the satisfaction of hearing him struggle with words.

"You're not taking anything I don't want to give, Joss." Still stroking him, I move back to his face, then trail my tongue along his jaw to his ear, working him with my hand. His breathing grows ragged and he fists his hand in my hair. Joss is on the verge of losing control, and I want him to. "

"You can fuck me if you want."

"Don't say that."

"Why? Don't you want to?"

Joss winds a hand into my hair and pulls my head back. I smile down at him, as he crashes his mouth against mine. He grabs my ass and his fingers dig into me, and I push his shirt from his shoulders, wanting his skin on mine, aching for more. Joss breaks away for a moment as he pulls off my bra, and our mouths are together again in seconds. His skin is hot, and my peaked nipples brush against his hard chest adding to the ache between my legs.

"You want me to lose control, don't you?" he growls at me.

"Maybe."

He sits and, grabbing me by the ass, he hoists me up, and I wrap my legs around his waist. His hard cock pushes against my clit through my jeans and I groan, hanging onto his firm shoulders. Joss spins me around and pushes the books on his desk to one side before lowering me, lips still on mine again.

Joss kicks off his shoes and we drag at each other's jeans, adding them to the pile on the floor. He pulls my legs to the edge of the desk and opens them; pressing against me, my panties a barrier I don't want. I make an soft sound in my throat and wrap a leg around his waist pulling him closer.

"You're fucking beautiful, Vee," he says and runs a finger along my panties. I suck air through my teeth, the material between me and his finger too much. Joss silently agrees, hooks his fingers around the edge, and pulls them down.

As I kick them off, my hand finds him again, and I run a featherlight touch along the shaft. Joss sucks in air, fingers finding my wet centre in response, then shoves me back onto the surface so I'm forced to let go of him.

Gazing down, Joss slides a finger along the seam of my sex and watches as he pushes a finger inside, his breath ragged.

I sink back, head against the cool wood. My chest tightens and breathing comes in short pants as he teases my clit with his thumb, sliding a second finger into me. "I'll do anything you ask, Vee, but that doesn't include destroying who you are."

He has to. Joss needs to let go, to allow his power to take over.

"I need you to show how you feel, Joss," I murmur. "I need to know you want me."

"Of course I fucking want you. I was waiting for you to want me." He leans forward and nips my bottom lip gently as he moves his hand, stroking the sensitive spot inside.

My heart swells again. "Always. I always wanted you. But right now I *need* you. This."

He rests his head on my shoulder, taking shuddering breaths. "Vee, I always wanted to go slow with you the first time, but I fucking can't." Joss places a hand on the table next to me, the restrained part of him fighting through.

"Don't then."

He slides along me, and as his mouth close over mine again, he thrusts into me, hard, taking me by surprise. I shift and grip Joss with my legs, feeling him filling me, our position pushing him against the spot that guarantees me a place in the stars. I grab a handful of his hair and pull his face up, grazing my teeth against his lip. He growls and pushes harder, more frenzied than I ever expected.

He slides a hand between us, and as soon as he pushes his thumb against my sensitive clit, he jolts the hardwiring that sparks my body alight. He watches my response, mouth parted, hooded eyes on mine, as I begin to unravel beneath him.

Joss covers my body with his, kissing and nipping at my skin. "I'm not going to lose control, Vee." His breath heats my ear. "You are."

I wanted Joss to starve me of emotion, but he's consuming my self-control and using it for himself. Instead, Joss now has the control I wanted to take away from him. I hold my breath against the wave building with each movement until I tighten around Joss and the shattering bliss hits.

I bite into his shoulder to stop crying out.

Immediately, Joss removes his hand from between us and grips my hips, thrusting into me harder and faster as I climax around him, pleasure pulsing through. Within seconds, Joss matches my release, pushing himself to the hilt before dropping onto me, hand wrapped in my hair.

No.

This isn't what I wanted or expected. Joss's love for me courses between us, pushing away his darker part I asked to starve me. Every emotion we share fills my body and mind; our bodies linked, intensifying the empathic power I share with him. At this moment, I am Joss. I experience every emotion as he does and hear every thought running through his mind. His heart beats against my chest as if it were mine.

Sex with Joss holds more than the intense physical need and pleasure; his love trumps his famine and prevents him starving me the way I wanted. With each guy, something good passes in an exchange and not the powers they use to injure and kill. Maybe I listened too closely to Logan, believed him too strongly, and there's no way I'll lose my humanity soon.

But as I lie with Joss, our breathing stilling as we cover each other's faces with kisses, the voice that whispered in the dark recesses of my mind speaks again. *If I fill myself with each power, I can fulfill what I need to be.*

I will be stronger than any of them.

8

Vee

Seth sleeps on the sofa, and I sleep with Joss.

Following our sex in his study, I'm calmer around Joss. The one I spent time with eating cake and walking reappears, but he also spends the night reminding me again and again of the rawer Joss beneath. The natural comfort between us returns, and I fall asleep exhausted in his arms, his playful banter echoing in my ears as he strokes my face.

He's not around the next morning, and within minutes, sleepiness snaps back to awareness. What will happen today when we speak to Seth? Xander's quest for answers won't allow him to leave this house before Seth gives them.

Stealthily I head downstairs, listening for voices, and only hear Joss's and Xander's in the kitchen.

"Ah, great, I didn't need to take the long walk upstairs with your coffee." Joss smiles and holds out a steaming mug as I walk into the room. "Made using your coffee machine, of course."

I gratefully take the mug and circle it in both hands. Joss crosses and places a kiss on my forehead as he runs the back of his hand down my cheek. "Okay?"

I nod, and glance at Xander who gives a slight smile and shakes his head.

"I'm fine. Where's Seth?"

Xander points towards the lounge with his mug. "Sleeping. Still." He yawns. "I could do with some sleep too. Long night."

"Did you sit up and watch Seth all night?" I ask. "Seriously? The guy's injured and terrified, I doubt he'll go anywhere."

"Sure. Just like the other day when he disappeared because we left him." Xander sips and watches me over the top of his mug. "Remember what happened when we were away?"

My heart skips at the double meaning to his question. He hasn't referred to what happened in the hotel room, since our anger spilt over into crazy sex. His attitude towards me has softened, but the walls have definitely rebuilt.

"When someone murdered his friend?" I reply. "Is that what you're referring to?"

Hi studies me intently. "Yes, Vee. That's what I'm referring to."

Xander often stands in this spot in the kitchen, which allows him the best view between the two rooms, and cranes his head to watch Seth. "I hope he's ready for some questions."

I set down my mug and pull open a kitchen drawer. I stashed a few personal supplies in here when I moved from my flat, including painkillers. The guys don't seem to need them, another example why I want rid of my human side, but Seth must do considering the wound on his arm.

Xander and Joss watch as I fill a glass with water. "What? I'm taking this to Seth."

Xander nods. "Yeah, maybe you should speak to him first. Reassure him I'm not about to hurt him. But if I find out he's bullshitting us in any way, he's in trouble."

"I think between us, me and Vee can detect if he's lying or how he's feeling."

"I heard you make a great team." Xander's mouth twitches in amusement.

Heat fills my cheeks, and I curse myself for allowing Xander to embarrass me with the idea he could've walked in.

"Did you want something when you were looking for me last night?" asks Joss.

"Just a chat, but you were distracted."

I ignore his pointed comment. "Maybe you could have that chat now." I head to the kitchen doorway. "Now Joss isn't distracted."

Despite my new ability to read people, sometimes it's impossible to tell how Xander feels. Can Joss? Xander's ambivalence to what happened in the hotel room is a relief because I worried what happened would cause more issues between us. I've a long way to go before he allows himself to fully accept my role.

Seth's asleep beneath a blue blanket in the darkened room. I open the curtains to a dull November day and stare in dismay at the rain clouds. Dreary weather equals dreary moods. I hate winter, but not only the cold. The sun rarely appears for months, leaving behind the autumn decay for a dark winter. Maybe a trip overseas with the guys would help.

Although god knows what I might come across over there.

Seth shifts on the sofa behind me. He takes his glasses from the coffee table and sits, immediately smoothing his hair. He winces as he moves his arm.

"I'm glad I saw you first when I woke up," he says in a hoarse voice, then clears his throat. "Though I'm worried about overstaying my welcome."

I hand him the water and painkillers. "Thought you might like these."

As Seth swallows the tablets, I sit on the nearby armchair. "What happened to Casey?" I blurt.

He straightens and stares at the glass. "I'd rather talk about that with your friends around. I don't want to tell the story twice."

"Okay."

"Are they around?"

"Xander and Joss are."

Seth immediately stands and brushes at his clothes. He peers down at his wounded arm. "I should thank them all for helping me."

"I think they'll expect help and answers in return."

"I'll help because I really need theirs."

I only know Seth from online, or the few times we met, and I'm cautious. I've never picked up lies from him, and his voracious need to uncover truth matches the one I had until a short time ago, but Xander's right about the question marks over him.

I chew my lip, desperate to hear his answers.

Who killed Casey?

And was he there when it happened?

"Can I ask you something?" he whispers.

"Sure."

"The guy. Did I see you..." He swallows. "Did you kill him? Was I hallucinating? My head is fucked and I can hardly remember what happened the last twenty-four hours." Seth clears his throat. "But when he held me against the tree outside his eyes looked bright red and he looked inhuman. I thought it was a joke and somebody trying to scare me, but now I don't know what to believe."

I search for the right words to respond with as Seth drinks, holding the glass in a shaking hand. "No. But the truth is more frightening than you think, Seth."

"More frightening than people wanting to murder every friend I have?"

I meet his eyes with a silent *yes,* and he drops his gaze again as he finishes the water.

"Okay." Seth eyes the kitchen doorway as if he's headed for a painful interrogation process. "Let's do this."

9

Vee

One or two guys usually stand when we hold discussions around the kitchen table, but I've learned that if they all sit, they're focused and serious.

Seth sits opposite Xander and Heath, beside Joss. Ewan and I sit at either end of the table. Before we spoke to Seth, I asked Xander to consider he's talking to a freaked out human and not a supernatural creature. He gruffly agreed to take the fact into account.

Their combined energy fills the room, almost tangible, charged by the suspicion about the sixth person with us. Sporting teams can fill a space with testosterone; this team project a mesmerising power joined by their physical presence. These Four were definitely created to appeal to people, because the effect on me when I'm around all four at once dizzies me every time.

"First up," says Xander as soon as we're assembled in our

strange meeting. "What happened the morning we came to look for you? Do you know where Casey is?"

Seth looks Xander directly in the eyes at his "down to business" words. "I didn't know she'd died until I heard you talking to Taron."

Xander flicks a look at me, and I nod. The truth.

He sinks back in his chair. "Fuck. Did you see anything?"

Seth rubs both hands across his face. "I don't remember."

Again the truth.

"You don't remember what happened, or don't remember who did it?" asks Heath. "Who attacked you yesterday morning? The same guy as last night?"

"No. When the men came into the hall, it was still dark," he says in a low voice. "At first I thought one of the guys was him." Seth points at Xander. "He was the same height and build and held the same aggression."

Xander straightens again and places his arms on the table, leaning towards Seth. "I don't kill humans."

"If you say the guy who attacked us was someone else, then I believe you. After all, you saved me last night." He rests a palm on his cheek. "There were two men—they broke into the hall, and as I switched on a light, one of them hit me hard across the face. He knocked me unconscious, and that's all I remember."

Joss shifts in his chair. "What did that guy look like?"

"I don't know. His face was covered by a black hood. All I know is he had bright blue eyes and was strong. I didn't have a chance to look at anything else before he knocked me out."

"Where did they take you?" Xander's eyes narrow.

"They dumped me in a dark room. I don't know where. They took my phone and car keys, and I had no clue where I was. All I could think about was Casey. And Verity. I didn't know what was happening."

"You can call me Vee," I say in a gentle voice. Despite his weak smile, Seth's fear isn't dissipating and chaos fills his mind.

Xander continues his interrogation of the poor guy. "Tell me everything you remember about where they kept you. Any sounds? Smells? What was around you?"

Seth rests his elbows on the table and places his head in his hands. "Nothing. Just darkness. A musty smell I guess, like a basement maybe? I was unconscious a lot of the time, and when I woke, I felt sick—like I'd been drugged." He takes a shuddering breath. "A guy in a black mask came in—maybe the same one—and injected me with something. I passed out again and woke up back in the hall. For a few minutes, I thought maybe I dreamt it all until I realised how much I hurt and saw the blood on the floor."

The guys look at each other as Seth stares down at the table.

Casey's blood.

"Why didn't you leave the hall then?" I ask. "Go for help?"

"I hadn't been there long when the guy arrived who attacked me, and you stopped him. I spent maybe ten minutes lying on the floor trying to find strength to do something."

"And you're *sure* he wasn't one of the guys you saw before?" asks Heath.

Seth shakes his head. "No. The person who attacked me yesterday evening, the guy Vee killed, was taller."

Xander chews his lip and we exchange a look. "Vee didn't kill anybody. You must've imagined that. Been semi-conscious, maybe. He died of something else."

THE FOUR HORSEMEN: GUARDIANS 63

"But I'm sure I saw Vee..." He trails off and holds his hands across his face. "I don't know what I saw. I don't know if this is the drugs, or what the hell is going on."

I can tell from Heath's silent communication with the others that they're not about to freak Seth out further with tales of vampires and demons. But he has to know. Seth needs to understand exactly who he's in danger from. And we need to figure out why. Since when did demons target human conspiracy theorists in such a public way?

"Do you trust us?" asks Joss.

He gives a soft laugh. "I don't have much choice. I was attacked twice in the same day. You didn't kill Casey; you're the lesser of two evils."

"We're not evil," growls Heath.

"I don't know what you are. But if Verity—Vee—trusts you then I have to accept you're okay."

"He doesn't know anything. He's telling the truth," I say.

Xander's expression shocks me, as if he wishes Seth wasn't. He wants answers about the situation, and Seth doesn't have them.

Seth chews a nail. "Casey... Is she definitely dead?"

"We never saw the body," Joss replies.

"So she could be alive?" Seth's face brightens with false hope, which disappears when Xander pulls an image from a file on the table. Seth looks away. "Okay. Probably not."

Ewan takes the photos Xander tore from the walls at the hall and slides them until they cover the table. Seth picks through them silently, paling back to the colour he was last night as he does.

"What do the words mean, Seth?" Xander taps on the image with the writing on the wall.

"It's a line from a poem," puts in Joss. "I thought I

recognised it, so I googled it this morning. Yeats. 'The Second Coming.'"

Heath snaps his head around to look at Joss. "Second Coming? What the hell?"

My mouth dries. I don't believe in the Biblical, but how can I deny the connection? These guys were mentioned in the Bible. Joss believes in Lucifer, that Hell exists and is where the demons come from. The room lurches along with my heart.

"The poem is allegorical," says Joss.

Xander drops the photo. "Use normal words, Joss."

"It's about the world being fucked."

Ewan laughs at Xander's expression. "Well, that's not exactly news to us."

"Yeah, but why choose words from a poem?" asks Heath. "The other messages were taunts. What the hell does this mean?"

"What does any of this mean?" I ask. "We've no more answers."

"I know the poem too," replies Seth. "It's about what happens when chaos reigns in the world."

"Again, not news to us," replies Ewan. "We spend our lives dealing with chaos."

"More than ever recently." Xander glances at me and away again. *Since I arrived.*

Seth chews a finger, and I catch a hint of something I don't understand crossing his mind. The anxiety is the prevalent emotion, but there's a glimpse of relief.

"Now we're together we can look at Seth's info." I gesture at the files. "We can compare what we know and discover who or what's behind the attacks. Can't we, Seth?"

"Uh. I'm still trying to get my head around Joss reading poetry."

Ewan breaks into a laugh. "Oh man, if you think that's the strangest thing we could tell you, you're in for a bloody big shock."

"I suspect so."

"And are you prepared to tell us what you know?" asks Xander. "In return for our protection against whoever wants to kill you."

Seth pulls off his glasses and rubs them on his shirt. He can't deny he's on somebody's hit list. "Yes."

Heath flicks through a singed manila folder. "Unfortunately half your information we salvaged is burnt, or missing."

"Yeah, I need to get hold of a computer hard drive." He places his glasses back on. "The files in the hall were print outs with decoy information. We hoped to fool people that we didn't know as much as we did, or that we were following the wrong leads. The real info is on the drive."

Xander looks down at his evidence. "So this is all bullshit? I almost burned my fingers trying to save this!"

"Most of it." Seth's voice remains monotone and cautious. Each time Xander's tone becomes hostile the guy's anxiety spikes. "There's some information encrypted amongst there, in case something happened to us and another cell managed to retrieve the files. If I'd disappeared, and Vee looked through, she'd find something I'm sure." Seth looks to me again.

"Where's this hard drive?" asks Ewan.

"Somewhere secure. I hid a key card to a storage facility in my locker at work. If anybody steals the card, there's no indication which storage unit they'd need to look in. And if they locate the right premises, they'll have over a thousand units to go through and with no idea what they're actually looking for. If we can get hold of the hard drive, that will help."

"What's on there?" I ask.

"Research. Downloaded files from Nova. Background on people." He glances at Xander. "On you all."

Heath narrows his eyes. "What kind of information?"

"Vee knows."

"Information about you all killing," I say.

"Did you tell him *what* we killed?" asks Joss.

"No. How was I supposed to tell him and sound sane?"

"We didn't kill your friends," says Joss. "Believe us. We're also trying to find the people who did."

"I don't have much choice but to believe you."

"Yeah, especially if you're asking for our help. You're not safe, Seth."

"I'm aware of that." He lifts his arm and cringes. "And I'll help you in return but I don't want to stay around once I've shared the information I have. I'll go overseas and join another cell. I'm not safe in this country."

"You won't be any safer over there," says Ewan. "I promise you that."

He straightens his glasses. "Maybe."

"What exactly do you research at Nova Pharm?" asks Joss. "What's so important there?"

He shifts in his seat to face me. "Vee, you know from dealing with us online which organisations are highest on our radar right now. Pharmaceutical companies are growing in control, and there's money being siphoned from them. John infiltrated Nova Pharmaceuticals. Once he suspected something was happening, I took a job there as a cleaner too and started to hack into the systems at night. I've information we haven't shared online, especially since your

Horsemen friend seems skilled at hacking into places he shouldn't." Seth flicks a look to Ewan. "Sorry."

"Go on," says Ewan, voice hard.

"We're not sure where this is going but we've hacked into accounts of people whose names we don't recognise as connected to the company. We were on the verge of joining some dots when the disappearances began. I don't think it's coincidence John disappeared shortly after he handed me the information. There are layers and layers of names and organisations. Once I have that hard drive, we can go through what I know. Do you have any names or suspicions?"

Good question. The Horsemen have been walking in circles since the deaths began, with two possible suspects. One was Seth, the other a powerful demon. I've spoken to Ewan about how carefully the demon hides himself, and where they think the guy is linked, but they thought the guy was out of the picture. If one of his many pseudonyms is amongst Seth's records, this could be a solid lead.

"We need to get hold of that hard drive, stat," says Ewan. "Did John have anything at work we might need to find too? Notes?"

Seth nods. "He has a duplicate key card to the same storage unit, but I'm unsure what else might be left at his work. I never went to collect his belongings. Casey was going to, but..." He trails off. "Yeah."

"Cool. We can do that too when we visit Nova Pharm," replies Xander. "Today. Seth, I want you with us."

"What? Why?"

"Because I think it's a good idea for whoever is watching you to see that you're with us now."

I watch for Seth's protest, but he sinks back in his seat, defeated. I have some idea of the trauma he's going through, but his life holds worse fears than mine. I'm relieved he's decided to stay because, if he left, he'd have Xander pursuing him as hard as those wanting Seth dead.

"And the other issue?" asks Heath. "Taron? We need to get to the bottom of that too."

Ewan taps the table. "Yeah, I'm gonna get into that today. I'll have a dig around while you guys follow up Seth's leads. We know who he works with. We don't have a lot of contact with them. No fixed address, but don't worry, I'll find them."

"Do you think these others are connected with the attempt to kill Seth?" I ask.

A small sound escapes Seth's mouth, and I fold a hand over his, and squeeze.

Ewan snorts. "I doubt it. You said he was paid a shit load for this? Like he'd share that job."

"I bet they watch each other's backs. You're right. We need to track the pair down and talk to them."

Xander touches his shoulder. "And the rune. Joss, can you look for that in your books?"

Joss salutes him. "Yes, sir."

"Give me the afternoon, and I bet you I find where Taron's associates are. You go with DoomMan and find his hard drive." He fixes his eyes on Seth, extends his arms, and cracks his knuckles. "I can't wait to see what he has for us."

I hold the same reservations about Seth as they do, but they have to understand what he's been through. Do they think he beat himself up? Paid someone to attack him? The Horsemen don't understand humans as well as I do, but treating him like this isn't nice or helpful. If he brings them information that helps, life should get easier for all of us.

10

Vee

Seth is reluctant to go with the guys unless I join them, which I understand and am happy with. I want to be involved. I'll be more help here than with Joss and Ewan. He's wearing spare clothes Joss lent him: jeans and a plain grey shirt to cover his injured arm. Arriving at his workplace dressed in torn, bloody clothes wouldn't be a good look. I sensed relief from Seth that he could change, after spending a long time in the shower.

Nova Pharmaceutical's huge complex isn't visible from the main road and is located close to a small town on the outskirts of London's main metropolitan area. Cheaper real estate and a ready workforce. Xander insists on driving, and when Seth enthuses about his Aston, that's the first time I've ever seen Xander smile at him. I asked why we chose the most conspicuous car. Xander's answer: he wants those who know the Horsemen to be aware they're onto them.

We approach along the tree-lined road and use Seth's card to enter the gates into the car park. At least a hundred cars surround us—possibly more—under the watchful eye of security cameras. We park close to the exit, but there's no point hiding Seth's arrival as it'll be registered on the system now.

The concrete and glass building has a 1970s look; a box like shape connected by windowed walkways. As the UK headquarters, the place takes up as much room as a whole street and it's bordered by a high fence securing it from the fields between the compound and the road.

Heath sits in the passenger seat running through notes Ewan dug up for us, while Seth sits in the back, slumped out of view and fidgeting.

"And you're walking in and pretending to be detectives again?" I ask, eyeing up Xander's T-shirt and jeans.

"No. No point. Someone will know who we are. Fae or demons will watch us sniff around and then probably send somebody to watch what we're doing after we leave. That's the usual process; it's almost predictable."

"Yep. Then we often kill the demon spy and things quiet again," says Heath in a matter of fact voice. "A show of strength by us, and everything calms down."

I pull at the seatbelt rubbing into my shoulder and stare into the dreary day. This isn't the usual state of affairs because they've no idea who they're looking for this time. And Heath knows it.

The four of us head into the glass lobby, where the bright lights contrast the darkening afternoon and shine across the gleaming marble floors. A woman sits at a small reception desk to our left, beneath the metal company logo stretching halfway across the wall above her. Elevators face us, and stairs sweep up and around to the left.

The atrium's glass ceiling is high, and our footsteps echo as we head to the reception desk to engage her in conversation while Xander walks by with Seth. They again use Seth's ID card to access the lift.

The girl behind the desk ignores me as she speaks to someone on the phone, and her pink nails tap on a keyboard in front of her. She reminds me of the Clone Club, all perfect hair and make-up. The call ends and she looks up, quickly assessing my outfit and pigeon holing me exactly the same way the Clone Club do.

"Yes?" she asks.

"I'm here to collect John Murphy's belongings."

She eyes me doubtfully. "Have you made an appointment?"

"I didn't realise I needed one." I swallow as if fighting back tears. "It was spur of the moment, I guess. Is that okay?"

"Do you know him?" she asks.

Heath approaches and rests an arm on the reception desk, switching on the smouldering look he saves for occasions he needs to charm girls. One he used on me early on in our relationship.

"Hey," he says, mouth tipping at one corner into a seductive smile.

The girl's disdainful attitude switches into interest and the smile transforms her face, as if Heath's the highlight of her day.

He probably is.

"I'm a friend of John's," he says in a low voice. "And this is his housemate, Casey. I'd be really grateful if you could help us."

She rubs her lips together, unable to tear her gaze away. Heath's turning on his charm to achieve what he needs, but his flirting niggles. I shuffle closer so there's no doubt I'm *with* Heath.

She rubs her reddening cheek. "I'll call his supervisor and see if he has time to accompany you."

"That's very kind of you uh...?" He gestures at her with his long fingers.

She pushes her chest out to give Heath a clearer view, and not just of her name badge. "Suzy."

I cringe at the sultry voice. Good grief.

"Thank you, Suzy. We'll wait over there." He gestures at a crescent shaped, leather bench seat beside a glass table, opposite. With one last smile to cement the deal, Heath places a hand on my elbow to guide me away.

We sit on the bench, below a framed poster of a past advertising campaign for a heart disease wonder drug.

"She didn't even offer her condolences," I whisper.

"She probably doesn't know who he is. Maybe thinks he's someone who was fired. Big company."

"You're very good at teasing the truth from girls."

Heath shakes his head. "That's the only reason I'd ever flirt with someone, Vee."

I attempt nonchalance even though jealousy clutches my chest. "It's fine."

"I wish you hadn't told her I was Casey. What if somebody asks me a question about her?"

"Didn't think about that. I just thought it might help."

Heath stares at his shoes as we sit in silence for a minute.

"Vee. Joss spoke to me earlier."

"Oh?" I ask in a light voice.

"He told me what you asked him to do and blamed me." He frowns. "I didn't mean for you to interpret my words that way."

"But it's true, isn't it? I need to become Truth."

Heath places a hand on my leg. "I love you how you are, Vee."

Even without my ability, I'd know he was speaking the truth.

Love.

He's never used that word before. I've seen my heart and soul in his eyes when we've been in bed, communicating in the moment that the connection between us is more than physical, but his words terrify me. Heath feels for me as Vee. Is Joss right? If I lose my human emotions, will I lose the ability to love them?

I'm choked by the realisation what I asked of Joss. Am I impatient? Should I just wait to become like them?

But I'm not like them.

"Heath..." I squeeze his hand.

Footsteps tap across the floor and a young guy approaches. He winds a lanyard around his fingers as he looks down at us, piercing blue eyes beneath slicked black hair. He's tall, wiry-framed and something about him screams one word: fae.

"Are you John's friends?" he asks in a smooth voice.

Perspiration breaks out on my back as the word no almost appears.

Heath replies as I struggle not to speak. "Yes."

The guy continues to twist the lanyard and doesn't offer a professional handshake.

I hastily stand. "Hello."

"I'm Kai, John's supervisor." A muscle in his cheek twitches as he glances between us. "And you are?"

"Heath." He keeps his voice low, eyes fixed on the fae's. I watch for a reaction. None.

"I've been waiting for you to visit." He flicks a gaze to me. "Casey."

I smile. Why did the guys ask me to do this? I can't lie here, so no response is better than well, 'no'.

"Terrible circumstances." He inclines his head towards the lift.

Heath stands too, and his look confirms it: obviously fae. We can't speak about this, as he's close while we walk.

The elevator doors swoosh closed behind us, and Kai uses his staff card to operate the before pushing buttons with pale slender fingers. "John sometimes talked about you, Casey."

Oh crap. "Really?"

"But as a friend. He never had any photos of you on his desk."

"Oh. They weren't close," puts in Heath. "Just friends."

"Didn't he live with you, Casey?"

I glance upwards and point at the numbers flicking up on the elevator screen. "This place is very big. A lot of floors."

"Mmm-hmm." Kai flicks the card across his hand, the rhythmic tap matching the numbers counting up. Heath answering all my questions arouses more suspicion than I'd like.

We step out into a grey-carpeted corridor and past an open plan area where desks are arranged in squares. Another uncomfortable reminder of my human past stabs. The room is smaller, but the drone-like workers stuck in their cubicles, surrounded by holiday pictures and photographs of loved ones, is an uncomfortable reminder of my old job and life.

"My office." Kai gestures towards a closed grey door with his name on a silver plaque to the left. His role: Executive Sales Manager.

He opens the door to a bright and airy room where a

desk containing a laptop takes up most of the space with a large leather chair in front. A wide window covered with silver metal blinds faces out to the car park. The moment we're all in the room, Kai closes the door and rests against it.

His demeanour switches.

"What the fuck are you doing here?" he snaps at Heath.

"You know why we're here." Heath pulls out a chair and sits. "And I can tell you're fae. Who are you?"

He waves the lanyard at him. "Kai Fielding. I'm trying to keep on the lowdown. Departmental visits by the Horsemen don't look good!"

"Who do you work for?" asks Heath.

"Nova Pharmaceuticals," he retorts.

"Who else?"

"Nobody."

"So why on the lowdown?"

Kai scowls. "I can't talk to you."

"Why?"

Heath and Kai stand off, and I remain by the door.

"Do you know someone called Seth?" asks Heath. "He also works here."

"Seth Marks? Yeah, I've seen him and John together."

"Really? Are you watching them?"

"I wasn't *watching* him. I just had my suspicions something was off about John's death, so I've kept an eye on Seth. This is my normal job. I'm not investigating anyone!"

"Nobody asked you about either of them? Any fae?" asks Heath.

Kai pulls a square cardboard box from the corner of the room. "Do you want his stuff or not? There's nothing interesting in there."

I peer inside as he drops the box on the table. His belongings barely cover the bottom—stationary, note pads, and a pencil case. There aren't any photographs; not even of a pet.

"If you're his supervisor, you'll have a record of where he went in the last few weeks." Heath unzips the pencil case and peers inside.

"Yeah. Nothing unusual about his travels either."

"Can we see?"

Heath passes the pencil case to me, and I look inside. A key card.

"What's going on? Why are you so interested in him? He hasn't any links to demons, I'd know about that."

"Ah," says Heath. "You're here to keep an eye on the demon element?"

"No more than the next fae. You know we work in most areas humans do, and tell our court when something is getting out of line. The fae authorities tell you; you deal with the problem."

Fae? So who was fae at my company?

"Not currently," replies Heath.

"Why?"

"We've had a disagreement with Portia." *Disagreement? That's an understatement.* "Are you working for her?"

"I don't 'work' for anybody, I just said. I work here, keep my head down, and if I see any trouble I report to fae authorities, just like the majority of us do. We keep out of this shit, as you know. So I don't like this visit. I don't want any links to the Horsemen; it's dangerous for me."

Do any fae cooperate? I understand the race like to blend in amongst humans, but surely it's in their interest to pay more attention to the supernatural war brewing around?

But he's telling the truth, something Heath wants me to communicate as our eyes meet. I nod my head to confirm.

"Can we see records of John's last few business trips?" asks Heath. "His death is suspicious. We think there's demon or vampire involvement. Your queen might be pissed off with us, but this still affects you. I take it you're living with your family in the middle of the human world somewhere? How safe are they?"

Kai hesitates, eyes troubled as Heath strikes a chord. He sits at his laptop and I glance around the room as he types and the printer whirs. "Here. He never submitted his expenses so I don't know if he attended or not. The police have his credit card and bank records, I imagine. Although, I take it you're not working with the police on this?"

Heath takes the papers, folds them, and places them in his back pocket. "No. We're avoiding involving anyone, apart from who we need to."

Kai snorts. "As if you could do anything unnoticed." He tips his head at me. "Hang on. Is she your mythical Fifth? Rumours are she made an appearance."

"I'm Verity," I reply.

"Truth? Another Horseman to think she can call the shots, huh?"

"Another to save your backsides!" retorts Heath.

"Look, I don't know what's going on here but I'd prefer you left before I come under scrutiny." Kai walks to the door and pulls it open. "I've told you everything I know and given you more than I should."

Heath and Kai stand opposite each other, Heath refusing to move, with a warning in his eyes. "If you hear anything else, I want you to contact us."

"Like I said, I'll contact the fae authorities. They can decide whether to pass information onto you or not. Don't contact me again."

Heath tenses. "For fuck's sake. Your fae pride will be the death of you all."

Placing a hand in the small of my back, Heath guides me towards the door.

"Verity?" I look back to Kai. "You need to brush up on your lying skills."

11

Vee

Xander waits in the car, along with Seth. I'm unsure if Xander won't let Seth out of sight because he's concerned he'll run, or if he's worried about Seth's safety.

Seth sits in the back and snaps his head around nervously as he hears our footsteps and voices. I climb into the back seat beside him, holding the open box on my lap. Heath joins Xander in the front. Seth pokes around in the box with his lips pursed and then sits back gripping the pencil case.

"How did you go?" asks Xander.

Heath pulls on his seatbelt. "We didn't find much info. His supervisor gave us a list of places John visited on recent work trips." He hands Xander the paper. "The guy was fae, by the way."

Xander's brows shoot up. "John was?"

"No. John's boss."

Seth leans forward. "No. His supervisor was Kai. There's a girl called Faye who works in accounts though."

Heath chuckles.

"I made the same mistake," I say to Seth. "He means fae."

He looks at me blankly.

"Fairies." Xander starts the car. "But not your pretty, winged ones."

"What the hell are you talking about?" Seth asks.

"Maybe Ewan's idea would work," suggest Heath.

"What idea?" I ask, irritated I've been left out of discussions again.

Heath turns in his seat. "Ewan thinks we should hunt and take Seth with us. Maybe he'll see not everything can be explained away."

"Hunt what?" Seth asks says in a guarded tone. "I'm anti blood sport."

"You're not vegetarian too, are you?" asks Xander.

"I'm vegan, actually. Organic. I don't trust what might be added to food."

"Oh hell," laughs out Heath. "You'll starve if you stay with us."

Xander turns the car ignition and the engine purrs to life. "No wonder he's a skinny pale dude."

"I am perfectly healthy," he retorts.

"Sure you are." Xander turns his attention to Heath. "Was the fae guy elusive?"

"Yeah. Nothing suspicious about him though. Nervous, avoiding questions, but they always are. Gave me this."

Heath hands over the paper to Xander and runs through our meeting with Kai. "Right. We can take a closer look at these companies when we get back." He holds the paper over his shoulder to Seth without turning around. "You and Vee look through the list. Anything suspicious?"

"Did you find Seth's key card?" I ask.

"Yeah. In his jacket, in the locker, like he said." Seth holds up his black jacket to show me and smiles. "I also persuaded Seth to stay with us for another day or two."

"Persuaded? Xander style?"

"He was polite," Seth replies, and Heath snorts. "Well, he didn't threaten me anyway."

"Lucky boy," replies Heath. "Maybe he likes you after all."

"What's the address for this storage facility?" asks Xander.

Seth gives Xander the address, which he passes to Heath. "Call Joss and Ewan. I want them to meet us there. Just in case."

With a nod, Heath pulls out his phone.

"Just in case, what?" asks Seth.

"In case we run into trouble. It seems to follow you."

Seth frowns at Xander's terse tone. "That's not my fault."

"Hmm." Xander leans across to turn on the car stereo. Loudly. Without another word, he manoeuvres the car to the exit, then pushes the pedal to the floor as we speed away from the secrets.

I pick up on his mood lifting for the first time in days. For once we're moving forwards and not backwards.

The storage facility Seth used is located an hour away, close to a motorway exit. The blue and yellow signage points towards a low building, held on an industrial estate amongst smaller industry. The brown, rectangular look seems apt for a storage facility and is located beside a unit advertising bathroom fittings.

We approach a barrier with an entry keypad; Seth swipes the card and we drive through.

A number marks each unit, and the external ones have metal roller doors. The car crawls along the roadway towards the building's rear.

"How long until Joss and Ewan get here, Heath?" asks Xander.

"Maybe another ten minutes."

The car falls silent apart from Xander tapping his fingers on the steering wheel.

"If you're expecting trouble, why don't we get in and out as quickly as possible?" asks Seth and opens his door.

Heath drags his phone from his pocket. "I'll ask them to wait by the car. They can watch for anyone else arriving."

There's nobody in the vicinity, on foot or in the car, as we follow Seth across the wet roadway towards the building. He hunches down, face covered by his hood and grips the card in one hand. Xander and Heath stand either side, surveying surroundings for surprise visitors. Nothing.

A grey door, flush with the smooth wall requires a card swipe and a pass code to enter. Once inside, I blink under the fluorescent lights and stare at a corridor lined with uniform metal doors. The place smells freshly painted, and as sterile as the interior looks.

Seth leads the way forward before taking a right turn and along another narrow corridor. Close to the end, he pauses and pulls the card from his pocket. The door opens into a concrete floored, cupboard-sized space that would struggle to fit two people in. A cardboard box marked with the name of a removals company rests on the floor, a rucksack beside it.

"What's in these?" asks Heath.

"A year's worth of notes and duplicates of anything important," says Seth.

I prise open the box. "There's a hard drive in here, is that the one?"

Seth takes it from my hands and turns it over. Small numbers are written in silver on one edge. "Yes. The rucksack isn't mine though."

"Whose is it?"

Seth shrugs so Xander crouches to unfasten the rucksack. He pulls out clothes. "A guy's and a girl's, judging by the mix."

Seth takes the T-shirt and looks at the red symbol printed on the front. "This is John's. That's a logo for a game we play."

"John left a rucksack here? Are any clothes in here yours?" asks Heath.

Xander blocks the doorway. "Is that it? You think you can bring us here, grab your clothes, and run?"

"You're kidding, right? How far would I get?"

"About two feet," replies Xander.

Heath pulls the rucksack away from the wall and reveals a shoebox tucked into a corner. Seth crouches down to examine the box. He runs his fingers along black text written on the lid. "This is new too."

"Do you know what it is?" asks Heath. "Is it safe to open?"

"Yeah. John left this. He's written our code on here." He gestures at a series of letters and numbers, then drops onto his backside and removes the lid. He carefully lifts an empty envelope addressed to Casey at her house, which he drops in alarm as he reveals what's underneath.

Heath pulls the small handgun out.

"Fuck! Not mine," replies Seth. "I don't know how to use one."

Heath turns the weapon over in his hands, and Xander reaches out to pick up two passports beneath the gun. "You think your friends were planning a trip somewhere?"

"Maybe." He pushes both hands into his hair and stares down in bewilderment. "I didn't know they were."

"They didn't get far, did they?" Xander flicks through the passports and studies the pages. "Casey by a different name." He drops it back into the box and turns the other image to face Seth. "Is this John?

Seth nods, jaw set hard.

"Did you know they had plans to leave?" Xander asks Seth

"No." Seth's face darkens, mouth turning down as he stares at the items in front of him. "I did not."

"Why would they leave without you?" asks Xander. "What did you do?"

"Nothing!" I recoil as Seth's shout echoes out of the door, and he flings the box to one side. "I don't know what's happening to my life anymore! I'm fucking sick of this!"

"Whoa, tiger," says Xander. "Calm down. Take what you want and let's go. I'm expecting somebody to follow us, and I'm not in the mood for a fight, even if you are."

Seth scrambles to his feet and brushes dust from his trousers, snapping back to his calm persona. They're right. He's odd. "Sorry."

I gather the belongings from the floor and drop them back into the shoebox, which I give to Seth. Xander picks up the large cardboard box, and his face is obscured by the size. Heath places the gun back into the shoebox and then grabs the rucksack.

Seth stares at the shoebox, face set hard, eyes distant. How does he feel about the discovery? I know little about his relationship with John and Casey, but this is a shock.

How isolated is he? Since he's been with us, he hasn't mentioned contacting any other friends or family.

"You sure you don't have a passport squirrelled away too?" asks Heath.

"I have one, yes, but with *my* name on. It's at my house."

"I guess they're smarter than you then," replies Xander. "They have false names."

"And a gun." Heath gestures at the box.

"Not anymore." Xander pulls the gun out and tucks it into his jacket. "I think I'll keep this. Let's go."

12

Joss

I rest against my car bonnet and look around as Ewan joins me. Miserable grey industrial estate meets miserable grey weather. I bloody hate winter. I yank my jacket collar higher against the wind.

"Did they say whereabouts they were?" asks Ewan. "It's a bloody big place."

"Nah. They said wait here."

"Fun times." He kicks at some loose tarmac with his boot. "What do you think about this Seth guy?"

"I'm not sure yet. Let's see what he comes up with for us. I don't think he murdered anybody though. I don't get that vibe from him; he's terrified right now."

Ewan's expression shows he isn't convinced. "I guess Vee trusts him. I'll see exactly what is on this hard drive; if there's anything incriminating, I'll wipe it."

Vee. What the hell is going on with her? The unease from her request won't leave, even though she's calmer this morning. I knew sex with her would be intense, and I was unsure what power exchange would happen, and I'm worried whether I took away some of what she wanted in the moment I lost control. She energised me; hell, I could've spent all night repeating what we did, addicted now I've had a taste. But Vee seems stronger too and more determined.

Was the only reason she came to me because she wanted me to attempt to drain her emotions with my power? Or was her need something deeper? I spoke to Heath, who shares my concern. Should I say something to Ewan?

Ewan makes the decision for me. "How does Vee seem to you at the moment? I know you and Heath spent some, uh, time with her recently. Is she okay after her breakdown?"

I gaze across the car park at the empty boxes piled by the skip and papers blowing across the car park. "Vee told me she doesn't want to be human anymore, and thinks I can starve her of human emotions."

"What?" I look back to Ewan's incredulous face. "Why?"

"Because of the breakdown at the hall. She feels she's letting us down. Vee thinks she can't fulfill her role until she loses that side of herself."

Ewan blows air into his cheeks and stares at the ground. "That worries me."

"Yeah, me too."

He side glances me. "Did you?"

"Did I what? Do what she asked? No, I bloody didn't, but saying no to her goes against everything I feel."

"You had sex with her though. What was that like?"

I scowl at him in warning. "Ewan."

"Jesus, no. I don't mean what it was *like*. I meant what

happened with your power. Did it trigger like Heath said his did?"

"Uh. I guess." I shift. "I feel more connected to her, and she seemed calmer since. Maybe I half did."

"So you think she took your power? Or you gave her it?"

"Honestly, Ewan, I was caught in the moment, you know. Can we stop talking about this?"

"Do you think she's had sex with Xander?" he continues.

I'm bloody sure she has. I'm not stupid; I know what I saw the aftermath of in the hotel room. It's odd they're still distant though. Xander's bloody good at maintaining his front.

"I'd lay bets he has. Why are you asking?"

"I just want to know what happened." He catches my half smile. "You know what I mean! What if something weird happens to her once she has sex with all of us?"

"I thought you'd dropped the 'Vee's trouble' thoughts you had back when she first arrived."

Ewan digs hands into his pockets. "Have you ever had a girl affect you the way she does? She can be in a different room, and I sense her. Not just sense her, but I'm drawn to find her. Touch her. Protect her. If she's too close, I have to struggle to think straight. Does that happen to you?"

I nod.

"And how she reacts sometimes—that crazy sex drive. She doesn't understand who she is, nor do we. Now you've told me this, I'm worried."

"Don't you start overthinking too, Ewan." A nearby car engine distracts me, and a blue sedan passes the security gates and drives further into the estate. I elbow Ewan in the side. "Just don't succumb to her charms if you're worried about what she'll do to you."

"No, Joss. I'm worried about what I'll do to *her*."

The car travels back again, driving slowly by the gates. With the car window up, I can't see the driver clearly, but I'd swear he's looking our way as he passes again.

Something catches my eye to the left, further along the roadway towards one of the facility doors. A tall figure, dressed in black, a coat flaring around his body. I straighten. Forget the car. "Ewan."

I grab his arm and point, but the figure has gone.

"Someone there?" he asks.

"Yeah. Come on." I stride away, down the small slope towards the door I swear I saw the guy walk through. If he was a guy. Ewan follows, and texts Xander as we walk. Numbers on signs outside the doors indicate where units are located. I halt outside the door the person walked through.

"Wrong number," Ewan says. "Xander said Seth's is 2698. This is 2500-2600. You can't get in without a card."

"I'll wait for the guy to come back out then. You wait up by the car in case this is a decoy and others arrive."

One thing I hate in life is the constant suspicion. We interact with people every day, but we look for sinister motives in normal activities. No wonder we have trouble trusting Seth. We could be stalking a guy going about his daily business unaware two of the Four Horsemen follow him.

Ewan walks away, and I rest on the wall by the door.

Another thing I hate? Hanging around waiting to see if I'll be attacked or not.

The door clicks unlocked and I straighten, ready to walk in as if I have business here. The heavy door opens and a man carrying a box almost walks into me. We perform the weird stepping side to side ritual, as we attempt to pass each other but end up standing back opposite. He wears a suit beneath the long black coat and a hassled look. I grab the door and apologise for getting in his way. As a typical English guy, he apologises in return.

Now we're close, I'm aware he's human and nothing else. I watch him walk away in the opposite direction to Ewan and our car. Where's his car? Still holding the door, I debate what to do.

A quick look won't hurt.

"Ewan!"

I gesture at the door, and he sets off back towards me as I walk inside to a sterile building. Rows of padlocked doors stretch before me. Pausing, I listen for other footsteps or the metal creak from a unit door.

Nothing.

I head stealthily along the corridor for a fifty metres or so, then jump, adrenaline flooding as the door behind slams shut. Hopefully that's Ewan, so I turn to head back to the entrance. As I approach, I pass a corridor on my left lined with units and swear I can I detect a sense of something odd. A movement catches my eye and a black shape shifts around another corner.

Weird. I close my eyes and focus. Not a demon but something unusual I can't walk away from without investigating.

"Ewan! Row 10!" I call then hurry after the figure, hand inside my jacket ready to pull my knife.

I round the corner at the end of the short passage and abruptly stop. The air shimmers in front of me, as if I'm looking at something underwater, and stretches from floor to ceiling. There's no unusual scent or sound, just fresh paint and Ewan's footsteps following.

A sudden, intense dread grasps me, and every cell in my body screams at me to run. Before I can back away to find

Ewan, the shimmering air moves forward, deathly cold where it hits me in the face.

I reel backwards, my head hits the smooth concrete floor, and I black out.

I'm lying, limbs stretched out in a star shape, chained. My skin burns in agony, and I lift my head to stare down at my naked chest.

I have no skin.

I'm bloodied and raw, and the fear intensifies the torture. I scream out, the tormented sound joining the wailing and shouting surrounding me, hundreds of voices crying in the same pain and fear.

Manacles hold my wrists and ankles, and as I pull, the metal rubs my raw skin and more pain careens through my body. Darkness surrounds me and I can't move my head or see where I am. Breathing against the pain, I manage to tip my head and my nose almost touches metal bars one side of me. I tip my head up again. Bars above me, just centimetres from my face.

How can anybody experience injury and agony like this and stay conscious? Each time I sink towards oblivion I ache for, a noise jolts me awake—screeching as if I'm plugged into headphones. Even unconsciousness is denied to me.

I pant out breaths, praying this is a dream and close my eyes again.

The cage shakes, and I snap my eyes open. Someone or something looks down at me; the figure obscured by the bright, white light surrounding it.

The figure speaks in a whisper hardly audible above the screaming around me. "I have a proposition for you."

EWAN

*F*uck.

Don't let him be dead.

I stare down at Joss's prone body, then spin 360 degrees attempting to find his assailant.

Nothing.

Nobody.

"Joss?" I crouch down and take his arm, searching for a pulse. His pulse beats at a normal pace, but he's ice cold, and I snatch my fingers away as his skin drags heat from inside me.

I could cope with the situation if it wasn't for the frozen terror on his face, his eyes wide and the expression running waves of chills through me.

What the hell happened to him? I passed a guy leaving, but he wasn't anything remarkable. He said hello and I searched his face for hints of anything out of the ordinary but didn't see any.

Was I wrong?

"Joss?" He remains prone, and I stand again. Focusing all my senses, I attempt to pick up anything other than the fresh-paint smell or the distant echo from other storage boxes opening and closing.

Nothing.

I push hair from my face and stare down. Do I leave him? Find Heath? He's alive, but for how long?

Crouching again, I place my hands on his shoulders and shake, the cool biting at my hands through the material. Joss's head snaps back as his chest arches upwards, and he lets out a huge breath. His eyes focus, but not before he pushes me hard in the chest and I sprawl backwards onto my arse.

"Get the fuck off me!" he screams.

"Fuck, man. Are you okay?"

Joss scrambles to his feet and looks down at his chest, patting, before studying his wrists.

"Joss. You're hyperventilating. Slow breaths, dude, or you'll pass out."

He blinks at me, but the fear I saw earlier remains. "Did you see anything? A demon?" He stares ahead and backs toward me.

"No. I haven't seen anything apart from a guy. What happened to you?"

Joss slides his hands down his legs as he bends over, heaving more breaths. "I don't know."

"You were attacked, and knocked out? Did you see who by?"

"No," he says to the floor. "There was something weird in the air, and it hit me. I don't know. What the fuck happened?"

"I heard you yell my name a minute ago and followed you. I found you on the floor. Are you hurt?"

He examines his clothes again, then drags off his coat. He yanks at his shirt and pulls it over his head. Wild-eyed, he moves his fingers along his naked chest and twists to examine his side. He turns his back. "Can you see anything? Please don't tell me there's one of those runes on me."

"No. Nothing. You're fine. What the hell happened?"

Joss puts his shirt back on, pale face reappearing through the hole. "I had a vision, Ewan. A fucking terrifying one this time." Joss squeezes his eyes closed and shakes his head. "I was somewhere. Trapped."

My mouth dries. "Somewhere dark?"

"Yeah." He opens his eyes. "I know we have visions sometimes, but I saw something, Ewan. I saw through the darkness."

I chew on a knuckle. I want to ask Joss what he saw, but a hundred times more don't want to know. I don't want to share whatever put the terrified look on Joss's face, in case he triggers a memory hidden my mind's dark recesses.

"Whatever happened, we need to get the fuck out." I grab Joss's arm, but he continues to stare into a space close by. "We can tell the others what happened."

The last thing we need is more freaky shit, but at least he's unhurt.

"I can't describe what or where, and I don't want to think or talk about it," he says in a hoarse voice.

But Joss won't have a choice, and even though I nod in agreement, he knows. I won't ask questions now, but the others need to know.

"C'mon, let's find the others and see if Seth has his info."

I'm no empath, but I know when someone's not in a good place. I walk out with a quiet Joss, followed by my fear whatever he saw might change him.

13

Vee

We return to the house with Seth's odd collection from his storage unit, including the gun and passports. Since he discovered them, Seth's returned to his mute behaviour, and the dark look that came over him remains.

At least we found the hard drive.

The moment we're home, Ewan pulls out his laptop while Seth sits with his shoebox on the table in front of him, and our afternoon trip is followed by an early evening working through the information held on Seth's hard drive. Xander's lifted mood drops again when we don't find anything useful as quickly as he'd like.

I don't know where Joss is. Ewan told me he's sleeping; I'm surprised Xander allows him to. Or I would be if I hadn't noticed the whispered exchange between Ewan and Xander once we arrived home. Something more happened to Joss than they're telling me.

"Mate, if anything on that hard drive fucks up my laptop you're gonna be sorry." Ewan narrows his eye at Seth, who gestures for Ewan to turn the laptop around.

"Nothing will happen, unless you have the wrong password. I'll open the files."

I smile to myself as Ewan hunches over nervously, as if he gave Seth his baby to hold. A fleeting image of Ewan and a baby crosses my mind; a scene I could never imagine happening.

"You want me to run through the info I have? Or did you want to look yourself?" he asks.

"Tell me what's on here." Ewan spins his baby back round and jabs a finger at the screen. "Uh. Why is there a file with my name?" His brow tugs deep. "Files with each of our names."

"I said we had some information on you. I can show you what, but please don't delete it."

Ewan sniffs. "It won't be true anyway. I told you reality isn't what you think."

"I'm beginning to see that," he mutters. "Could I have a pen, please?"

I slide a notepad across to him, and he writes a series of neat letters and numbers. "Here're the passcode for all the files. What's inside is self-explanatory. We researched each department and the board, and all our findings are there. We couldn't join the dots, but if you know some of these names and who they're connected to, it could help?"

"Why couldn't you join the dots?" asks Xander.

"Because someone covered their tracks. Each time we hacked into the system, the information began overwriting by something else unrelated. We couldn't keep up or download quick enough."

"Whatever you did find was worth murdering you for," mutters Ewan. "Why?"

"I don't know. There are secret projects, but we can't identify what. At first we thought it could be illegal drug trials, but now we think they're bankrolling something the board are trying to hide."

"Like what?" asks Xander.

"We never found out." He pushes the notepad across the table to Ewan. "Look, I'm not going to lie to or hide anything from you; this is all I have. Now you have everything, can I leave?"

Both Seth and I know the answer before anybody speaks. "That's not a good idea," says Heath.

"I feel like a prisoner with twenty-four-hour guards," he complains. "I just want out of the whole situation."

"Do you honestly think that's possible?" I place my hand over Seth's. "We'll help each other."

Seth pulls on his lip and doesn't reply.

Ewan clicks through the files and leans forward to study the screen. "Leave this with me. Let's see what's in here."

For the rest of the afternoon, Ewan, Seth, and I remain in the kitchen scrolling through and comparing data. Ewan tells Xander to leave the room; his constant hovering annoying us. He disappears to see if he can find more information about who Taron worked with.

Ewan runs through connections Seth's made between Nova Pharm and smaller companies, but there're no names the Horsemen have come across before. He spends hours combing through the information, checking names again and again, but the linked companies and people are new to him. Some have only existed a few months—months when they were distracted looking for me.

Ewan makes a list to check off, but there're dozens to work though and we won't manage this in one night.

"I don't understand why we've never come across these people before," says Ewan as he returns from Joss's study with more printed sheets.

"We can't know everybody, Ewan. They work fast sometimes."

"No, but we're fed information from the fae a lot, and we keep up to date that way."

The true consequences of the screw-up between the fae and Horsemen becomes more apparent. I've held conversations with the guys about what they can do to reforge their alliance, but not in Xander's earshot. They're at a loss what to do, and I'm acutely aware I'm part of the problem.

If saving Portia's life a few weeks ago isn't enough to cement their relationship, I don't know what is. Heath suspects somebody is influencing her, but I can't see how anybody could manipulate Portia.

Seth stays with Ewan, who barks questions at him occasionally, and I stay with them both to help comb through the information. My head aches with frustration, and Seth's dark-rimmed eyes and tired face tell me he's not faring well.

Eventually, Xander returns with Heath. "Fuck this. Let's work on the other issue. Ewan, did you find anything out about Taron while we were at Nova Pharm?"

"Yeah, I have found more on Taron. I managed to hack into his bank accounts; he may've been a great assassin, but he's not good at covering his tracks. I've pieced things together and found most of his clients via their bank accounts, but this latest amount has come from an offshore account. A tax haven. There's no way I'll hack into that easily or quickly. The best I can do is hit the system with a virus to prevent anybody touching anything in the records until I do."

Xander crosses his arms. "So what *have* you found?"

"A contact number for his friend, Syv."

"Oh?" Placing his palms on the table, Xander looks down at Ewan's scrawled notes. "Her address?"

"No."

"Then how do we find them?" asks Heath.

"Easy," replies Xander. "We phone her."

Heath takes the paper from Xander. "Oh yeah? The Horseman can randomly contact dubious supes and expect them to say yes to a meeting?"

"Not us. Him." Xander points at Seth.

Seth straightens. "Me? I'm the one with a target on my head!"

"Obviously you don't tell her who you are," sneers Ewan. "Just say you have a job for her and want to meet."

"What? And she'll agree to meet me? Just like that?"

"Offer a crap load of cash, and she'll be there. Tell her it's a big job that needs two people, and she'll bring her mate, Abel. Then we'll have both of them in one place."

All four guys look at Seth who rubs his nose and pales. "But why me?"

"Because we're asking you to," says Xander in a low voice. "Do you want us to help you or not?"

"How? By calling their 'dial-an-assassin' number?" he asks snarkily.

"Yeah. You leave your details, and they'll contact you."

"How do you know all this?" he asks. "Have you used them?"

Xander laughs harshly. "Do you really think we need to use other people to help us?"

I want to step in and ask them to stop being so bloody rude to Seth, but I can also understand their urgency. Xander shoves the paper at Seth who clutches it as if he's been served a death notice.

"Ewan, since you hacked into Taron's life, can you find info about his other clients?" Xander asks. "If there's any connection between them?"

Ewan taps the table. "I can't figure out who they all are, but so far no. Most of his recent assignments were "solving" petty gang wars between shifters who wouldn't stick to their patch, or the occasional demon who needed to eliminate another. I think Seth needed taking out quickly because whoever did this knew he was with us."

"That's bloody great!" exclaims Seth. "I told you I should leave. I'm not safe with you all."

Heath ignores him and points at Ewan's notes. "Have you checked all the Nova Pharm board backgrounds? Are any connected to Taron and his mates? Any demon we know of?"

"Yes. I have names, but there aren't any red flags that any are demons. Some are fae. It would be a lot easier if..." He trails off and cocks a brow at Xander. "Well, whatever, this will be harder to piece together on our own."

"But the fact no demon names are coming up *is* a red flag. We *know* demons rank high in every organisation. The corpses showed obvious signs of demon interference," replies Xander.

"This is driving me bloody nuts!" exclaims Heath. "Every step forward, something else is thrown our way. Why isn't anything showing up yet?"

"Calm down, this will all be connected somehow. We'll

solve this." Ewan touches him on the shoulder. "Once we speak to Syv and Abel we'll have some more clues."

"You reckon?" snorts Heath. "Even on the creatures that attacked Ewan? How are *they* connected?"

"Don't worry about them," says Xander. "We can deal if we come across them again."

"But they weren't normal enemies!" says Heath. "In case you didn't notice, they killed Ewan in seconds. What if I hadn't been there? What if I'm not with you next time?"

"Heath. Chill."

Heath's expression darkens, and I swear he's about to hit his brother. I know we're having problems dealing with all this, but I never expected Heath to snap.

"I think we're all tired," I say in a soft voice. "I know you're superheroes, but you can't keep going forever, even fuelled by beer."

"We're not superheroes, Vee," growls Heath. "We're not guaranteed to save the world like in the stupid human fantasies."

"Heath. Dude. Calm down. Come on, let's take a walk." Ewan stands and attempts to take Heath's arm.

Heath violently pulls his arm away. "She's right. We're tired. I'm going to sleep, let me know when you need me to get back on the stupid fucking merry-go-round."

The door slams as Heath leaves, and heavy footsteps stomp upstairs. Xander focuses on a sheet of paper in front of him, and Ewan doesn't respond. I look to Seth who's studying, and rubbing, his injured arm. A small smile plays on his lips.

14

Vee

I intend to talk to Heath, but when I reach the upstairs hallway, I spot Joss's open bedroom door. He sits on his bed, staring out of the window with his back to me. I thought he was resting?

I sense something's wrong—I did the moment we met up outside the storage units because he barely said a word and struggled to hide panicked emotions. He spent time in conversation with Xander, and the guys left Joss with me and Seth as they checked out a different area in the facility. When I asked Joss why he didn't go too, he pointed at Seth and smiled. But something in his eyes remained distant.

Joss doesn't move when I walk into his room. Only when I stand between him and the window does he look up. His face matches Seth's for tiredness, exhaustion lines drawing his face. He regards me with dull eyes and forces a smile.

"I thought you were resting?" I ask.

"Nah, I just wanted a break from everything."

I sit on the bed beside him and take his hand. "You're cold. Are you okay? Do you guys get sick?"

"No. Must be the weather."

I place a hand on Joss's head and move to cup his cheek too. Cold skin. "Tell me the truth, did something happen earlier?"

He moves my hand and places it on my knees. "Nothing serious. I thought I saw someone or something when I was checking out the storage place, I passed out and Ewan found me."

I take his hand again. "Joss! Why didn't someone say something?"

"Because it's nothing. We looked and there was nothing there. I must be tired, and my mind's playing tricks."

Joss swallows and blinks rapidly.

Hmm.

"Don't lie to me, please, Joss," I say in a quiet voice.

"I'm not. I genuinely thought I saw something weird in the air around, but Ewan didn't. I was a bit dizzy, maybe overtiredness?"

I can't imagine a Horseman suffering a dizziness to affect him like this. "Fine."

"Vee..." Joss touches my face with cold fingers. "Sometimes I have weird dreams, and my mind plays tricks on me. We've been on the go for days, maybe there is a point of exhaustion we reach, and the dreams joined the daytime."

Is he trying to convince me or himself?

"Was it me?" I ask. "Did us having sex do this? Did I hurt you?"

Joss laughs and holds my face in both hands. "Far from it. You know that."

I hold his face in return and place a soft kiss on his mouth, but he pulls away. "I think I'll rest."

Joss is exhausted, but there's more happening here. I can't feel the same affection he had for me the night in his study. This isn't like Xander's deliberate closing down, but as if his interest in what's happening around him is buried.

"Maybe you'll feel better if you do. Xander has plans to meet up with Taron's friends later. You might need your energy."

Joss swings his long legs around on the bed and settles back, hands laced behind his head. Toned abs peek out from beneath his T-shirt and I bite down the desire to explore them again. Joss on the bed? Tempting.

"Tell him I'll be down when I feel up to it." His words and closed eyes shut down any chance of following my thoughts through.

"Talk to me if you need to, Joss," I whisper and kiss his forehead. "I'm worried about you."

"I will."

He doesn't open his eyes.

He will talk to me, whether he likes it or not. I know something's wrong. I'm pissed off nobody told me everything about the incident, especially after Xander's words about not hiding things. I guess that doesn't include me. I grit my teeth. We need to work on the trust issue - on both sides.

My thoughts turn to Heath I shake my head at the situation. They love and care for me, always ready to step in if I need anything, but I do the same to them. I've seen them interact as a family unit rather than four guys sharing a house, and I add something different to the dynamic. I've become the glue holding them together; I'm not something to break them apart. Hopefully this will be accepted soon.

Loud music pounds through Heath's bedroom door, and when I knock, he doesn't respond. Another one who wants his own space.

Tired and stiff after the days on the go, I grab my towel and head to the bathroom. I pull open the shower screen and turn the taps full, watching the steaming water pour down as I strip.

Bliss. I close my eyes as I stand beneath the water jet, inhaling the soothing scent of my lavender and geranium bodywash as I lather myself. The house has a bath, and I often eye it up dreaming of bubbles and long relaxing soaks but haven't had a chance yet.

The bathroom door opens and someone walks in. Annoyed, I rub steam from the shower screen glass to see who's invading my privacy.

Heath. He stops, hand on the door, and we stare at each other. There's no disguising I'm in here since I'm plainly obvious through bubble-streaked glass.

"Heath! I'm in the shower."

"I can see," he replies. "You should've locked the door."

"You should've knocked." Water continues to run down my hair.

The shower door opens and Heath grins at me. "Sorry."

I splash water at him. "Sorry? You apologise by not leaving and instead take a closer look?"

Heath rubs the water from his face and draws a leisurely gaze from my breasts to my mouth. We've shared a shower before, and the memories dance happily into my mind as I attempt to stay cross with him. Impossible, especially when he pulls his T-shirt over his head revealing his too-hard-to-resist body and the promise of a repeat performance.

"I'll leave if you want." The water continues to trickle, and I stare back, lips parted. "Or I can join you?" He unbuttons his jeans. My pupils dilate and my nipples harden as he continues his slow steady look that tells me every intention.

"Depends what mood you're in. I'm unwinding from the stress and conflict downstairs." I push wet hair from my face.

"You could put me in a better mood?" he suggests, hands still on his fly.

Heath, the guy who does crazy things to my body when we're in the same room and even crazier things when I'm in his arms, stands half-naked offering me more of a favourite addiction.

I move towards him and curl a damp hand around the back of his head to pull his face closer. "If you make it worth my while," I whisper.

Heath laughs in a too cocky way as he slips out of his jeans and steps into the shower. He winds an arm around my waist, drawing me against him. I wait for a soft kiss, but the water splashes as Heath slams me back against the tiles, his hard mouth closing over mine.

My soapy body slides against his chest, as he pushes me harder into the wall, and kisses me deep and hard. My face smarts as his growth scrapes across my face, my lips swelling at the ferocity of his kiss. He lifts me and pushes one of his legs between mine, brushing against my slick centre. I grasp his shoulders and dig my nails into his skin as he grips beneath my legs, hands on my backside, as he circles his tongue around my breasts, teasing my already peaked nipples.

I grip his shoulders harder, and he looks up at me, the smug smile growing.

"I'm sure I can manage that," he replies.

Water drips from his flattening hair and touches his lips. He licks the drops away, and the water plays over us as he assaults me with another toe-curling kiss. Heath slides his hand between my legs, and his mouth parts, his eyes filling with lust, watching my response as he strokes me. He pushes a hand against my sensitive sex, thumb on my clit, and I close my eyes, relishing the chance to fall away from everything happening outside this room and in our crazy world.

I grasp his hair in one hand and our lips meld, hot breath mingling. Heath swipes his tongue along my lip. "You taste so fucking good, Vee."

The water runs down around us, and however hard we try to hide from the outside world, I know it isn't far, for long. "Don't stop."

"No chance." Heath roughly turns me around, and I almost slip before righting myself and pressing my hands against the wall. My head tugs back as he winds my damp hair into a ponytail around his hand. I lose my footing again, and he drops my hair, winding a strong arm around my waist to steady me.

Heath's erection presses against my back, and the ache between my legs becomes unbearable. I push back against him, dipping my head forward.

"You're so fucking beautiful, Vee." He slides his hand between my legs again. "So fucking wet for me."

He circles both my wrists in his other hand and holds my arms above my head, against the tiles, nipping and sucking at my skin along my neck and shoulders. He positions himself behind, and I shiver as I feel the tip of him against me.

Heath guides himself into me, and I tip my face upwards to the water pouring down on me. I can forget every other moment that happened today, every stress, every complication, and hang onto this perfect one with Heath.

15

Vee

After spending more time than I anticipated in the shower, I return downstairs to catch up on what's happening. Xander and Ewan are still in the kitchen, Xander standing behind Ewan, watching him work.

Xander looks around as I walk in, his face brighter than when I left the room. Some of his tension has washed from his face, but the tiredness remains.

"Seth came through. He's set up a meeting with Syv and Abel."

"You look surprised," I reply.

"They must be short of cash since they're happy to meet at short notice."

"Whereabouts?"

Xander looks back over Ewan's shoulder. "The Warehouse, 10:00 p.m."

My stomach lurches at his words, and I can't help but

glance at Ewan. His brow furrows, and he nods at me. I shake away the human reaction. No way can anything like that happen to me again; I'm a million miles from who I was that night.

"Where is Seth?" I ask.

Xander points at the lounge without looking around. Seth sits in the same spot on the sofa every time I see him in the lounge, lost in his own world, as if sitting there keeps him grounded. Joss must sense Seth's unhappiness and worry, but does nothing to help him. Joss who still hasn't emerged to help. I asked Heath if Joss was okay, and he brushed me off in the same way Joss did. Following our sexual connection, I pick up Joss's emotions more readily, and I'm concerned how that's faded today.

"Are you ready for an exciting night out?" I ask.

"Oh yeah, meeting assassins, that's just awesome." He adds to his sarcasm with a thumbs up.

"At least you found some different clothes in your backpack."

He's changed into black jeans and a T-shirt with a symbol the same as the one he said was John's. It's unfamiliar to me—a semi-circle in a grunge pattern with a cross in the middle, red on a black background. I'm sure the guys will notice and, like me, wonder about the significance.

He brushes at his tee. "Yeah. A bit creased."

"I'm sure the guys will lend you an iron."

"You think?"

Omigod, that was a joke. He doesn't think the Horsemen possess an iron, surely? And why would anybody want to iron a T-shirt?

"They'd probably just hit me with it." Seth points at his cheek. "I have enough bruises."

"Seth, I don't think they'll hurt you."

"I know, Vee," he says. "I do feel better when you're with me, but, man, those guys scare me."

My heart goes out to him. I have some idea how he feels, but the guys told me the bizarre truth from day one. My idiosyncrasy meant I accepted what they told me, and Seth's gradually forced to do the same, confronted with a reality he cannot deny.

"They don't usually allow people into their lives," I say. "They're suspicious of everybody."

"But they allowed you."

"I'm connected to them."

"How?"

"It's a long story."

"The best stories always are. But I know you're safe now, and that matters to me, especially after what happened to the others in the group." He rubs his hands on his knees and studies me. His pale blue eyes distract me because they're an unusual contrast to his pale face and dark hair, and often filled with an uncertainty he tries to mask.

"I'm sorry about Casey," I whisper. "That must've been hard."

He looks away, at a spot on the wall above the TV. "I try not to think about it. Part of me hopes she might still be alive, but that's not likely, is it?"

"Never say never in this world."

We lapse into silence, and Seth fidgets with his jacket zip. "I wish Ewan would return my laptop. Or phone. Or anything really."

"Finding it hard to be unplugged, huh?"

"Yeah. There're people I want to contact, you know? I think the guys are trying to stop me."

"You're welcome to borrow mine any time."

"I will. Thanks." He pauses. "Mr Friendly says he'll take

me to my place to pick up some gear so I can stay here. Do you think I should?"

"You know that's a good idea," I say softly.

Ewan wanders in, and Seth tenses. He's wary around Xander, but seems genuinely scared of Ewan. Considering his size, tattoos, and general taciturn nature, I don't blame him.

"I hear you wanted your laptop?" Ewan half drops the silver laptop onto Seth's lap. "Some interesting info you had on that hard drive."

"Yes, it's good we found some connections, isn't it?" I ask in an attempt to diffuse. "Very helpful."

Ewan chews his lip and drops the hard drive on Seth too. "I'm glad I had a chance to look at your research. Do you have backup files?"

Seth smoothes his hair and flips open the lid. "Those *were* the backup files."

"Cool." He digs his hands into his back pockets as he watches Seth plug the hard drive into the laptop. Seth's key tapping becomes more insistent, and he mutters under his breath as he rapidly moves through files and screens.

"What the fuck?" He glances up at Ewan. "What did you do?"

"Removed some information."

I look over to Seth's screen. "What information?"

"Removed? You've corrupted the fucking files!" growls Seth.

Whoa. I tense expecting an aggressive response from Ewan; I bet he's waiting for the opportunity to attack. Instead, Ewan regards him, and his mouth hardens. "You had a lot of shit about me and the guys on there. I don't want that spread amongst your conspiracy buddies."

"But how did you manage? These files were protected..."

Seth pushes both hands through his hair. "Months of research gone! Not just our investigations into you."

"Oh, don't stress, I have the important parts on my laptop now. You don't anymore, that's all."

Seth holds his temples with his forefingers and chants under his breath, "Do not react."

"Ewan," I say. "Was that necessary?"

He looks at me and runs his tongue along his teeth. "He tried to fuck with the Horsemen, and Pestilence has special skills, remember?"

Seth drops his laptop on the table and shoves it away from himself before sinking back and staring at the ceiling. I glare at Ewan and his smug smile turns into a frown. "What?" he mouths at me.

"He hasn't crossed you! He bloody helped, Ewan."

"Yeah? Then why store files about us on there? Hardly a friendly move."

"We didn't know who you were," protests Seth. "We log anybody who's suspicious."

Ewan narrows his eyes. "We? Who's the 'we' digging info on us?"

"My dead friends!" I blink at Seth's loud, harder tone, praying this won't spiral into an argument. "So don't worry. Nobody else has information about the people you murder."

Ewan takes a step forward and looks down at him. "Don't cross me, or you'll come across worse viruses than the ones on your laptop, mate."

Does Ewan hear Seth mutter "fuck you" under his breath?

I pull a disparaging face. With a shrug, Ewan heads out of the room followed by a glare from Seth.

"Well that doesn't help our trust issues, does it?" he snaps.

"The guys are very protective of their lives; you should understand that, Seth."

"Hmm." He flicks his fingernails as he stares ahead.

My curiosity gets the better of me. "What information exactly did you have on them?"

"Like I said, murder victims. Their movements over the last few months. Their background."

"Background? How far back?" I glance at the door in case Ewan is still around.

"Not far enough. I think they changed their identities a few years ago, and I'm sure they'll do it again."

"Ten years?"

"Something like that. But we—I—will find out who they really are." He side glances me. "Sorry, Vee. I know they're your friends, but I trust them about as much as they trust me."

"Maybe that will change." I force a bright smile.

Maybe, but not any time soon.

16

Heath

We sit in silence on the drive to the Warehouse, Vee in the back of the car with Seth and Joss, Xander beside me. Ewan chose to ride his bike again, but this time tails me rather than driving away to take his "scenic route." I heard Seth complain to Vee, he's exhausted over the last few days; I forget how frail humans are. Yeah, I need sleep, but I can keep going as long as needed. In the past, we've worked 24/7 on cases, and not even ones as important as this one. I'm wired after the last few days and eager to keep going too. My anxiety rests as much with the threat to human life, and not just Seth's. This is big, otherwise Xander would calm down for five minutes.

I'm still not coping with him trying to follow a hundred leads at once. I'm unable to get my head around dealing with Nova Pharm at the same time as the assassin issue. Sure, they're probably connected but man I'm confused by all this. Hopefully Ewan can straighten this out, join a few more dots, and we'll have a clear direction. This had better include whatever the hell those things are and how they're connected to the chaos swirling around us.

Tonight will be a start, or another dead end to infuriate us all.

Joss isn't a great help right now. He's either feeling overwhelmed as I am, or something more than he's admitting happened earlier today. Ewan told me he'd found him unconscious, and Joss was unsure what happened. Ewan didn't see anything unusual, and there was no sign when we left him outside to check over the place too. Joss doesn't usually imagine these things, so what the hell happened?

Xander strides through the crowded entrance, into the bloody awful music, and pushes his way downstairs to the motley crew writhing on the dancefloor with Joss hot on his heels. I'm bemused by Xander pausing in the middle of the crowd who've parted around him as he stands hands on hips surveying the room.

Vee hangs back in the entrance hall with Ewan and Seth. She doesn't seem keen on a return visit. Ewan holds Vee's hand and dips his head to talk to her, as she looks at the floor. My concern and need to protect draw me back over there too.

"Everything okay?" I ask.

Vee straightens and nods, but I don't miss her glance at Ewan. Seth chews a nail and edges toward the wall. I'm guessing not his usual hangout.

"Xander's heading up the other stairs." Ewan points at Xander's tall figure halfway up the metal steps opposite.

A girl bumps into him on the steps and stops to apologise. It's hard to see her face from a distance, but the strobe lights pick out a slender figure and short dress. In the past, Xander would've placed a hand on her arm, responded to the inevitable flirting with his hot self, but today he doesn't pause.

Yeah, whatever he says about her, Vee's changed him. I'm interested to see if his random hook-ups continue, or whether his respect for our new dynamic will stop that.

I'm sure if he gets a taste of Vee, he won't want to look anywhere else again.

Joss told me his suspicion about Vee and Xander, but I can't believe anything happened. Xander's adamant he won't succumb to her, as he puts it, and the tension remains between them. Perhaps he's a little softer around Vee, but I can't see him giving in to how he feels yet.

I tip Vee's chin and kiss her softly, my body immediately firing at her sweet scent and taste, evoking memories of our time in the shower earlier. She strokes my cheek with the back of her hand, and the smile she gives indicates she's having the same memories.

"Come on," Ewan says.

Seth hurries to walk next to me as we push downstairs through the revellers and up the stairs Xander took. Xander and Joss already located a table at a smaller bar area and sit on the cushioned chairs.

"What are you doing?" I ask.

"Let's have a drink while we wait," says Xander.

Ewan and Seth sit too, and Vee lowers herself into a chair, hesitantly. "Do we all need to stay? I'd rather wait outside."

"You'll be okay, I told you." Ewan places his large palm on her leg, and she shuffles closer. What's this about?

Seth leans closer to me and says in a low voice, "Being here pisses her off because of what happened last time."

"What do you mean last time?"

Xander asks if I want a beer, and I nod. No surprises when Seth declines for a glass of sparkling water.

"When we walked in, I heard her talking to Ewan about the last time she came here with him. Someone spiked her drink or something. I couldn't quite understand what they were talking about."

Huh?

"She said something about not wanting Ewan to find her being assaulted again, and that if anybody tried, she'd rip their head off," continues Seth. "Man, she's full on sometimes. Not the quiet, nervous girl I expected."

What the actual fuck?

Seth's eyes widen. "Oh. Crap. Did you not know?"

My darkened expression answers his question, but that look isn't for him. I squint at Ewan and Vee through the dim. Secrets? Why the fuck didn't Ewan and Xander say something happened to Vee that night. Since when do we hide things from each other?

One beer and ten minutes spent fuming later, I ask Ewan if I can talk to him. Privately. The confused guy follows me to a quieter spot, the edge of the bar, and I lean my elbow on the sticky wood.

"What's wrong, man?" he asks. "Have you seen something you want to hide from Seth?"

I suck my teeth and weigh my words. A guy, spiked black hair and piercings, approaches the bar and I shuffle further along.

"Tell me why you never told any of us that someone attacked Vee the night you and Xander came here before."

He straightens. "How do you know about that?"

"Was Xander in on this decision? Did you both hide this?"

"No. He doesn't know either. Vee wanted me to keep it between us." I swear under my breath. "Heath, it's done with. Nothing serious happened."

"Tell me exactly what happened," I growl. "You don't hide this shit!"

"Calm down, man. It's nothing."

"The hell it is," I growl. "I am so fucking pissed off with you. Tell me *exactly* what happened."

Ewan runs me through a staccato list of events that night, and Vee's vehemence around killing demons in the days that follow now make more sense. Am I pissed off because Ewan and Vee hid this from me, or because Vee didn't tell me? At the time, I thought we had a closer relationship than the others, back when I fooled myself she was the human chick who'd fallen for me, the guy from work. I soon realised we'd never be that, and the bond extends between all of us, but the fact she never confided in me hurts.

"You told nobody?" I ask. "Why the fuck not?"

Ewan drags a hand through his hair. "Vee was upset. Confused. She was still trying to come to terms with everything, and I decided keeping it on the lowdown might be a good idea. Maybe some of it was worry how you guys would react, especially you. I don't know. The whole situation got weird."

"How?"

"The incubus looked like me so everything was more complicated. I wanted to forget it happened too."

"But we don't fucking do this!" I growl. "We never hide shit."

"Really? You think Xander's always straight down the line with us, such as what he does when he pisses off on his own?"

I inhale. Maybe Ewan's right, but right now this is what matters to me.

"Look, I'm sorry, okay? Just don't be shitty with Vee about this."

I shake my head. "Oh man, wait until Xan finds out. You need to tell him and Joss. No more secrets."

I wait for Ewan to protest but he tips his head acknowledging he needs to fess up. Didn't he realise we'd discover what happened eventually?

In silence, I order more beers and attempt to switch back to this evening's task. But I can't help the hurt that remains.

17

Vee

As the evening passes, my nervous memories of the place do too. I'm not that naive girl anymore; I've proved that to myself repeatedly. I focus on tuning out my emotions, something that comes more easily since my time with Joss.

Joss checks his phone. "They're late. Where are you meeting them again, Seth?"

"Syv said she'd text me when they get here. So, maybe you should give me my phone?"

Joss shifts to reach into his jacket pocket. Seth holds out a hand for the phone, and Joss pauses. "Dude, my friends are mostly dead. All the ones in this country anyway, and I'm on a wanted list. Who do you think I'm gonna call?"

Joss drops it into Seth's hands. "Fine."

As Seth examines his phone, Xander and Heath return

from their latest trip to the bar, drinks in hands. Xander slams two bottles down and foam overflows from the necks.

"Whoa," says Ewan. "Don't waste good beer."

Without a word, Xander shoves a glass of mineral water towards me.

"Thanks," I say.

He responds by picking up his beer and drinking heavily, refusing to meet my eyes. Wow, what's his problem?

"What if they ask me to leave with them?" asks Seth. "Is it safe?"

"I wouldn't recommend getting into a car with either of them," replies Heath.

"We'll be watching." Xander drains his bottle and nods at Seth's phone. "Any message?"

He shakes his head.

"Shit, they'd better arrive."

"Oh, they will," says Ewan. "After the amount of money we transferred to them, they'll be here to find out how to get the rest."

"Do I have to see them? Can't you? What if they grab me?" Seth scrunches a nearby paper napkin in his hands. "Their friend tried to murder me! Please..."

"He has a point," I say.

Heath rubs his head. "Nobody will hurt him in here. Maybe you should sit on your own for a while, Seth. Once they arrive, we'll join you."

"I could sit with him?" I suggest as Seth's eyes fill with more fear. Ewan and Heath glance at each other. "What? It'll be safer. I doubt Syv knows who I am."

Xander rests back in his seat and props his feet on the table. "Are you sure you don't want Ewan to join you both? He could make sure you're both safe."

"They probably know who he is," I reply but there's

something harsh in his tone. Figuring out whether Xander's moods are due to stress or rudeness can be tricky sometimes.

"Fine." He watches as Seth and I stand. "Just don't move out of sight."

"No chance of that," replies Seth, echoing my thoughts.

We head to a small table in the opposite corner, away from the bar and stairs. Seth obsessively checks his phone, not talking to me. A few minutes staring at the couple at the adjacent table, and Seth drops his phone on the table as if it burnt him.

"They're here."

"Do you know what they look like?"

"No. Xander said Syv's tall and um... memorable looking." He folds his arms tightly across his chest. "Your friends had better be close by. What if Syv and Abel stab me or something? It's dark in this corner, anything could happen."

"Seth. It's okay. I'm here."

He rubs the corner of his eye. "Right."

"Try to sound convinced!" I say and nudge him, but the deep lines on his worried brow remain.

A woman approaches, tall and dressed in leather pants and a matching jacket cinched at her tiny waist. Her sleek figure and fluid movements are feline, and she weaves through the people between us without touching any. The woman draws interested glances from the crowd—from both guys and girls. Her long, auburn hair is loose around her shoulders, and she scans the room, lips pursed.

"Omigod, why doesn't she just wear a neon sign saying, 'I'm an assassin.'" says Seth. "Look at her."

I'm too busy watching the guy who's with her. He's tall too, though not quite as tall as the guys, and wiry in the way that hides a deceptive strength. His shoulders are hunched as he also takes in the people round him. The pair have matching jackets, matching attitudes.

Seth waves at them.

Actually waves.

I grab his hand. "I don't think that's necessary."

They approach and without a word pull out stools and sit. I fight looking back over to the guys; it won't take this couple long to spot them if I do.

"Are you Jimmy?" asks the woman. Her voice is silky and seductive, mesmerising Seth straightaway as she fixes her deep-brown eyes on him. She moistens her plump lips. "I'm Syv."

He nods. The guy crosses his arms and rests them on the table, sizing us both up. I do the same. His dark hair hangs into his eyes and touches the sharp cheekbones in his pale face. He purses his full lips before pointing at me. "I'm Abel. Who's this?"

"A friend," I reply before Seth can.

I look to Seth and pray he sticks to the story Xander gave him.

"Right. I'm not hanging around here. What was it you wanted?" asks Syv. "This sounds urgent. That costs extra, you know?"

"We have a job similar to one Taron had the other night," Seth says. "We can't contact him so thought you might want the work instead."

"What job?" asks Abel.

"We need you to help us solve a problem."

The woman laughs and taps her fingernails on the table. "That's clear as mud, sweetie."

"So, you don't know what his last job was?" I ask.

"Nope." Abel tips his head. "You can't contact him, huh?"

"No. We're a little upset that our associate chose the wrong person for the job. We're hoping you won't let us down."

"Yeah, he sure did," replies Abel. "Taron's not the most reliable person."

"Did he tell you what he was asked to do?" I ask.

Syv taps her index finger on her lips. "Firstly, we don't share information, and secondly you know the answer if you're connected."

Someone approaches the table—four someones—and they surround us. Abel swears and jumps to his feet, but he has no way to leave the area.

Syv remains collected, and her eyes jump from guy to guy. "Ha. Good. I hoped this was really you."

Heath frowns. "What does that mean?"

"Oh come on, who else likes to catch up regularly to tell me not to be a bad girl?" She smiles slyly. "And how often do you think we reply to mysterious strangers, whose names we can't trace, and meet them in clubs?"

"I'd presume that's your usual method," says Joss. He pulls a stool to sit at the table, and Ewan does the same.

"Wrong," replies Abel. "What the hell is this forced meeting for? We operate with your understanding. Why this shit?"

"Taron broke the agreement," growls Xander.

Syv smiles up at him. "Ah, my magnificent War. How are things since we last met?"

"Difficult, and we need your help, Syv."

"From us? You're scraping the barrel, aren't you?" asks Abel.

"Taron's assignment was to kill a human," says Xander, eyes fixed on Syv's.

Her face remains impassive. "That's why he's missing, I presume? Did you deal him some Horseman retribution?"

"I was hoping you'd know why or who hired him."

"Didn't you ask Taron before you finished him off?" she says with a laugh. "You're usually good at extracting information." She flicks her fingers at me. "Now you have Truth as well."

I straighten. This woman knows her stuff, but what did I expect? I want to join in the conversation, but don't want to give Syv any clues to the sort of person I am. I'll be happy if she walks out of here thinking I'm a weaker girl under their protection.

"He died before we could. Someone had cursed him." Xander pulls out his phone and flicks across the screen. "Do you know this symbol?"

Syv looks as he hands her the phone, shakes her head, and passes to Abel. He pulls a face and shrugs. "No clue. Demonic?"

"Joss can't find anything similar in his books, or online."

"Ah well, sucks to be you," says Abel.

"I think you'll find it sucks to be *you*," retorts Ewan. "We need info."

Syv nods at him. "And how, dearest Pestilence, are we supposed to give you info we don't have?"

"You must know something! You three work together."

"Loosely. We don't exactly have an appointment book or share a diary. Mostly, we don't discuss anything we do. Isn't that right, Xander?"

Heath stares at the side of his brother's head for a few moments, and his surprised look worries me. Has Xander a relationship with these people the other guys aren't aware of?

Xander leans down, palms on the table, and into Syv's

face. "I want a list of your recent jobs and contacts. Both of you. I want to know any detail Taron may've let slip about his assignments recently."

Syv doesn't flinch. "Taron's been laid up. He had a particularly nasty run in with a shifter. The other night was his first job for a month."

"How do you know this?"

She fixes her eyes on his. "He stayed at my place."

"Then you must know who contacted him," replies Ewan. "Think."

She runs a finger across the back of Xander's hand and smiles at him. "All four of you in our faces? Large sums of money in our bank account? This is serious shit. I can think more carefully, but it might cost you extra."

Xander snatches his hand away and the pair are nose to nose. I've seen him aggressive to guys, but never a woman, and I'm uncomfortable he is. But this isn't a human woman, but something else with her beguiling behaviour. What is she?

"If you don't tell us, it might cost *you*."

They remain in stalemate for a few seconds, Syv's eyes glittering before she looks away to Heath. "Did *you* kill him, Death?"

"No, we told you, magic."

"And are you going to kill me?"

"No. But I don't think we'll be the only ones who want to ask questions."

Syv leaves a deliberate silence before she looks back up. "May I speak to you alone, Xan?"

I tense. *Xan*. She's familiar. Maybe too familiar.

Xander steps back and gives a curt nod. The woman stands, unfurling herself like a cat woken from sleep, and she smiles at me in a deceptive way; a sweetness disguising a poisonous opinion. "Your new companion is fascinating."

Heath immediately takes her vacated seat, ensuring Seth is still penned in and I watch, stomach churning as Xander talks to Syv.

"How well does she know him—you all?" I whisper to Joss.

"Well enough to know not to cross us."

"And her and Xander..." I trail off, annoyed I betrayed my jealousy.

Ewan barks a laugh. "No. Xander doesn't screw demons."

I snap my head around to look at her again. "Demons? What? I thought you killed demons!"

Abel laughs. "Half demon."

"Half demon, half what?" I ask.

"No idea. And she's not a fan; she doesn't have the powers they do. Syv relies on her physical ability to kick people's asses."

I hold my hands out palms upward in a confused gesture. "Heath?"

"We don't know what Syv is. Nor does she."

The three of us—misfits," says Abel to me. "These four know how that is. We steer clear of the pure races. Especially demons and fae." He gestures at himself. "Vampire, exiled due to lies by my Elder. Luckily not dead."

"Oh."

"Yet," mumbles Ewan.

"Jeez, thanks, mate."

"You all live day to day. Look at what happened to Taron."

"Yeah, if he was mixed up in dodgy shit that's his call. I stick to simple jobs."

"And nobody contacted you with a harder one?" Heath asks.

"Not me."

"Syv?"

"Like she said, we only share so much info."

I can't take my eyes from Xander and Syv. I'm intrigued by his body language. His threatening stance has loosened, but in the dim, their expressions are hard to make out. Neither lie about their connection to Taron's assignment, but there's a guard up in Syv that I can't penetrate, as if her mind is fogged.

Through the whole exchange, Seth remains silent, focusing on sipping his drink and avoiding eye contact. What the hell must he think about our conversation?

Syv walks away from Xander, in the direction of the exit, and Ewan echoes my thoughts. "What the fuck? Did he let her go?"

Xander returns to the table and jerks his head to one side while looking at Abel. "You can go too, but I suggest you watch your back."

"I spend my whole life watching my back," he retorts as he stands. "Including whether you four are behind me." He nods at Seth and me. "Look after yourselves."

Abel blends into the crowds and leaves the six of us in silence.

"Xander?" asks Heath. "What the hell was that?"

He shoves his hands into his pockets. "I don't want to discuss some things in front of other people. I'll talk when we get home. There's nothing else we can do here."

Does he mean Seth or someone else? Because that comment was spoken with his eyes on me.

18

Vee

We head back to the house, with no explanation from Xander about the outcome of his conservation with Syv. Halfway home, Xander turns his music on at a volume to confirm he doesn't want to talk, a favourite trick of his.

The moment we enter the house, Xander tosses his keys on the table in the lounge and Seth drops onto the sofa and rubs his face.

"Are we having a meeting about what Syv told you?" I ask Xander.

He shrugs and walks past me, and I stare after him. *Rude.* If they have a meeting without me, there'll be hell to pay. Seth sits quietly. Is his mind full of stories about demons and vampires? Wondering if we spiked his drink?

Joss nods and studies me with an expression I'm

uncomfortable with; he's not happy either. "What's happened to make Xander grumpy?"

"Xander-ness." He heads after him. Do I follow? What the hell is happening here?

"I get the hint they don't want me involved in situations unless it suits them." Seth picks up the neatly folded blanket and pillow from the end of the sofa. "I'm tired anyway. They're an odd group of men."

"You already know that."

He removes his glasses and polishes them with vigour on his T-shirt. "Are you in a relationship or something? You know, all five of you? Is that how you knew them?"

"Some of us are," I say. "Was it water you wanted?"

I've never needed this conversation with anybody human, and I would've found an explanation strange if anybody had the conversation with me a few weeks ago. I'm certainly not comfortable talking to a guy about this. What if he thinks the situation applies to every male in the household and he can join in?

I look back at the softly spoken guy whose acceptance of the situation grows. He just sat in a bar talking to odd people and one said he was a vampire. Friends of someone he witnessed me decapitating. Xander keeps a close eye on Seth, but would he leave if he had the chance? Is Seth used to being on the fringes, the way I was, or are there friends and family looking for him?

"Are you okay sleeping on the sofa?" I ask.

"I'm fine." He lowers his voice. "I'm not sure I'll stay around though, Vee."

"I want you to Seth. I don't think you're safe."

"I don't feel safe anymore. Anywhere."

I reach out and squeeze his hand. "Everything will work out."

"Will it?" he whispers.

Seth follows me to the kitchen where he pours a glass of water. We're under Xander's silent scrutiny, and I ignore the rude bastard. Seth says good night to him, which is polite considering their mutual distrust.

Xander quietly closes the kitchen door and rests against it. "Spill, Xander," says Joss. "It pisses me off when you hold back."

He rubs his nose. "Syv says she's seen that symbol before, but can't remember where. She thinks it's an ancient magic that few know."

"And *she* just happens to know?" asks Heath and arches a brow. "How coincidental."

Xander shakes his head. "Syv's job involves retrieving magical items people want; she sees a lot that's hidden from most. She thinks we need to talk to the Collector who's one of her biggest clients. Syv says she can get us an introduction, but that threatening him won't work."

"Well, that leaves you out," laughs Joss. "I guess you'll need to wait outside the house."

"Ha bloody ha." He pauses. "She told me she has a list of Taron's regular clients and is prepared to sell them to us."

"What the fuck?" growls Ewan. "She has a bloody nerve."

"We're running short on time and options," snaps Xander.

Heath pulls on his bottom lip. "How do you know she isn't bullshitting you, Xander?"

"Because Syv won't risk what happens if she crosses us. I think her self-preservation and greed wins in this situation."

My tired head can hardly cope with this. "Who's the Collector?"

"Fae dude," replies Ewan

"But won't he refuse to talk to you because of Portia?" I

don't look at Xander. I don't want accusations I'm slyly digging at him.

Xander rubs a hand across his mouth. "'Fae dude' is a huge understatement. He's older than Portia, older than any fae in this world as far as we know. Possibly immortal. He was one of the originals who escaped just before their realm became unliveable. He doesn't bother with the hierarchy the fae created in the human world and couldn't give a crap about Portia's little empire."

"And why is he called the Collector?" I ask.

"He collects things." I throw a beer cap across the room at Joss and his sarcastic comment, and it bounces off his head. "He pays for artefacts and books, and has a collection some would kill to get their hands on. Demons and fae have both tried to get him onside, but he won't budge."

"And—surprise surprise—the fae don't trust him," puts in Xander.

"I can imagine why if he keeps company with assassins. Is he looking for something in particular?" I ask.

"Not sure. Mostly anything brought through from his realm. As one of the originals who escaped, he also has the strongest magic."

"He'd be dangerous if he gave a shit," says Xander. "But he's self-serving. Plus fae and demons? Not happening. You've seen how fae would rather keep the status quo."

Heath perches on the table edge. "Yeah, he's watched one world destroyed, maybe he can help us stop the same happening to this one."

Xander shakes his head. "I don't think things are at that stage yet, Heath."

"Right. So we pay him a visit tomorrow?" asks Joss.

"Tomorrow?" Xander digs hands into his jacket pockets. "Tonight."

"Shit, no way," replies Ewan. "C'mon, man, we've been going non-stop for days."

"I don't want anybody else killed."

"And what if we make mistakes, Xander?" says Heath in a low voice. "We can only keep going for so long. Our bodies are human, even if we're not."

I look at the dark sky outside the window. Why does Heath need to remind me of that?

"Okay. I'll go on my own."

"Xander," says Heath in a warning tone. "Don't."

He jerks his head at me. "Vee. Tell them. You're the one who wants humans to stop dying."

"Yes, but it's almost 1:00 a.m."

"You can't see him without an appointment anyway," puts in Heath.

Wow. This guy must be something if the Horsemen need to make an appointment to see him.

"I don't need to rest." I step back as Xander pushes past Heath and walks to the kitchen door, then wince at the noise as he exits and the door slams.

"You don't think he's going, do you?" I ask.

"Nah. He left his car keys in the lounge."

"At least he's walked away," says Joss. "He can walk off this angry energy he has, because it's building too high right now."

"Should I talk to him?" I pause. "Don't do that!"

"What?"

"The looking at each other because you're hiding something."

Heath makes a derisive sound. "Who wants a drink?"

"You just said you were tired." I gesture at him as he pulls out the whiskey bottle.

"Just a night cap. Ewan? Joss?"

"Yeah."

The guys' quick drink becomes several more "quick drinks". I'm part of them, but sometimes prefer to be out of the "guy stuff." There's also something uncomfortable here, a different tension to the one that has followed us around recently.

"I think I'll head to bed; I expect Xander will drag us out the door in a few hours." I make to leave, but Ewan catches my arm.

"I need to talk to you," he whispers.

Oh no, not another lecture over what I asked Joss to do. "I'm tired. Can this wait until tomorrow?"

He huffs. "Fine. But find me as soon as you wake up."

Leaving Ewan with the promise I will, I head upstairs, not paying attention to my surroundings and almost trip over Xander sitting on the top step.

"Why are you there?" I ask as I step past him. "I thought you went out?"

"I'm calming down." He doesn't look up. Xander's long fingers grip the stair he sits on, and his hair's mussed as if he's been pushing his hands through. There're plenty of other places he could sit, why here? "And I need to talk to you about something."

Not another one. "Okay..."

"Vee." He stands and faces me, and his mouth thins. "Why didn't you tell me what happened to you the last time we were at the Warehouse?"

"Oh." *Shit.*

Xander bites down on his lip, a trait I've noticed when he tries to hold back anger, but his harsh tone betrays him. "I know you were attacked. I'm pretty damn pissed off with Ewan, but I outright asked you if you were okay. Why lie to me? *How* did you lie?"

My heartrate ticks up at his building anger. "I just evaded the question, remember? I was embarrassed and didn't know how you'd react. I didn't want anybody to know."

"But I was there to protect you, and I failed."

I tuck a strand of hair behind my ears. "You didn't fail. Ewan was there for me and—"

"And you wanted him to help, not me?"

"Is this jealousy?"

"No, this is pissed off. This is you coming between the four of us."

I stiffen. "What?"

"We swore you wouldn't, but we never kept secrets before. Now, because of you, Ewan did. Things are shaky enough without you causing problems."

I swallow hard as a familiar anger builds to match his. "I'm not having this conversation with you, if you're going to attack me like this." I keep my tone as calm as possible and walk into the bathroom.

I grip the sink and take deep breaths. Why accuse me like these things? He's seen the extra power I bring to the situation. Okay, maybe Ewan and I should've told the others, but I wanted to forget.

The thoughts tumble around my mind as I brush my teeth. Xander and I were calmer; our battle in the hotel room brought a new equilibrium. Now this.

I walk out to find Xander outside Heath's room, resting against the wall. I sigh. "Xander. If you have an issue about this, can we talk about things with Ewan around too? With all of us? I agree, we need to address the situation, and I apologise for not telling you."

A muscle ticks in his jaw and his scowl remains. Seriously? I calmed down and apologised, but he's not apologising for his unwarranted accusation?

"Good night," I say.

He doesn't move to allow me past him, and my arm brushes his on the way into Heath's room. I try hard, but I can't help sniping when he doesn't respond to me. "Grow up," I mutter under my breath.

Shock takes over as Xander half-shoves me into the room and slams the door behind him. "What the hell are you doing?"

"Talk to me, Vee."

"Back off," I warn.

"Tell me why you both lied to me."

"Because I didn't like or trust you that night!"

He snaps his head back as if I slapped him. "You don't have to like me, but you need to bloody well trust me."

"I do. Not then, but now."

"Like or trust?"

"Trust. I can't comment on the *like* part."

"Is that right? You seemed to like what I did to you the other day." He moves closer and looks down at me, and the anger in my veins switches to a different feeling as he stares at me openly for the first time in over a day. My heart thuds, cheeks heating at his silent scrutiny. "Didn't you?"

"Don't go there," I whisper. "Don't start that again."

He holds out a hand to touch my face, and I push it away, so he seizes hold and drags me towards him. "I'm angry, and I'm fucking hurt, Vee. Do you know how many days I spent on my own looking for you? Has anybody told you that?"

"No."

"Where do you think I was when you first arrived?" His grip on my hand tightens. "I was halfway across the fucking country searching."

"Why? Heath worked at Alphanet. He knew who I was."

"There were other people out there who we thought were 'Truth.' I followed false leads over and over again until Heath told me he'd found you." He pauses. "For weeks, my whole life centred around finding you. Nothing else mattered."

I stare back at the mixture of hurt and anger held in his eyes. "I didn't know," I say in a quiet voice.

"They fucked about, and you almost got hurt. But *I* started the search. *I* found you existed."

I attempt to pull my hand away, but his grip remains tight. "And I'm not what you expected? Is that your problem?"

"I never expected to react like this around you. I thought after we fucked the other night you'd be out of my system, but the opposite happened."

I reel at his choice of word, at him belittling what happened between us to something that insulting. His words wrench my heart as if he'd pushed his hand into my chest and grabbed hold himself. "You arsehole."

He drags a hand down his face. "You're fucking me up, Vee. Sometimes, I think maybe Logan's right about you and—"

At the mention of Logan's name, power rushes through me and takes over. In a reflex move, I yank my arm away and slap Xander's face

The slap is harder than I intended, and I wince at the smacking sound. "Don't you fucking dare!" I hiss at a stunned Xander. "Don't you dare accuse me of that too."

He touches his face and moves closer again. I cringe away in case he returns my attack. "How do you explain what you do to us? To me. I'm watching them lose focus because of you."

"Shut up," I hiss again.

"It's true. Look at me. I lose control around you. I can't think straight. And for what? For you to pick and choose who you ask for help?"

"That was once! You're the one causing the divisions. Look at how your decisions screw things up. Portia. How you react to me. You're losing your grip and desperate for someone to blame other than yourself."

I smack him in the chest, and he stumbles at my strength.

"How can you talk about trust and say things like this? You're hurting me, Xander. How can I talk to and trust you if this is how you treat me?"

"Because this is what you do to me. Each time I'm around you, a part of me screams out to connect with you and take away the frustration and anger."

"You're contradicting yourself now," I growl.

He seizes hold of me again. "You matched me; you didn't yield, and I can't... Just can't."

"Can't what? Cope?"

Something else pushes through Xander's anger and pulses toward me.

Fear.

But what scares him? Me? Himself? His loss of control in every situation recently?

"Stop being selfish and understand how this is for me," I say.

He drops his hold and steps away; in his eyes, there's an awareness he's pushed too far and shown too much. "I'll see you in the morning."

I suck in a breath as Xander walks away. *Actually fucking walks away from his problems. Again.* I stand, at a loss over what happened, and listen to the low voices downstairs. Surely others heard that commotion?

I sit on the edge of Heath's bed, trembling after the encounter with Xander. This is why we stay apart. This is why I haven't approached Xander before to talk about what happened. Every fight with Xander, each look or touch, passes the raw passion he holds. With him, I don't need the spark caused when I use my powers, because the flame is always burning.

Screw this. He's right.

I can match him.

I stride into Xander's bedroom. He's shirtless, the light through the open curtains illuminating every glorious square inch of his defined chest and abs. He pauses in his undressing, fingers at the belt of his jeans. Xander may have removed his shirt, but he still wears the darkened expression from a few minutes ago.

Before he can react, I walk straight over, grip his hair, and push my mouth onto his. Xander responds in kind, one hand tangling in my hair and the other around my waist. I close my eyes, breathing him in, inhaling the memories from the last time we connected. Gripping my hair tighter, Xander kisses me deeply and snatches my breath.

Usually when we're close, his need to stay distant keeps us apart, but when we touch, it's as if our bodies react instinctively. The way his lips move, how his tongue strokes mine. His touch. Our bodies are tuned to each other, and that will never change.

I'm not fuelled by my powers in this moment, but by the need for Xander's touch. I want his skin against mine, and that touch to take away the ache that builds every time he rejects me.

I unbutton Xander's jeans as he pulls the buttons on my top, our mouths sealed in an unrelenting kiss. He breaks away for the briefest moment as he pulls off my shirt and throws it to the floor. Our lips and bodies connect again, and I drag my nails down his chest to his waist. I pause and meet his eyes filled with a burning intensity to match the heat of our skin.

The fervour from our fight before remains, but this time our short, sharp breaths aren't hurtful anger. Our walled up need is ready to break through. Continuing to look Xander in the eyes, I slip my hand inside his jeans and wrap my fingers around him.

Our teeth collide, tongues battling, as the hunger for each other grips us. The mint taste from brushing my teeth mingles with Xander's, a powerful reminder of the last time we clashed. My breasts push against his hard chest, peaked nipples brushing sending shivers across my body and heat between my legs. I move my hand along his hard cock. Xander groans into my mouth, and he pulls away, mouth parted in pleasure.

There's no fight for control here. I have it.

As if we already synchronise after one time, our clothes land on the floor in the same way as the hotel room. This time he doesn't get to hold me to the wall.

I push Xander, and he falls back onto the bed, eyes dark and curious. I'm on him before he can move, straddling him, aware of my slick heat sliding against his hard length pressing between my legs. He inhales sharply and grips my backside

No words.

I splay my palms across his chest, which rises and falls rapidly beneath them. He draws a finger along my stomach, triggering vibrations from my belly downwards. I lean down to place my lips on his; Xander runs his tongue along my bottom lip and I part my mouth, launching back into a battling kiss.

Pulling back, I hold his broad shoulders, pushing him against the bed. Xander's strength matches and could outweigh mine, but his hooded eyes and lazy smile taunt me he's in control of himself. Looking down at him, I reach between us and slowly lower myself onto him.

I watch for surprise on his face, but none shows. He grips my ass, and I rock my hips, lost in the sensation of him filling me as I move.

Our gazes lock, I drag my hair over my shoulders and continue to slide against him, luxuriating in the pleasure rising with each movement as our urgency continues. I steady one hand on his chest, riding him as I hold his other hand over my clit. He matches my thrusts, refusing to look away from each other. The connection to him forges again, and I tip my head back, eyes closed, mouth parted feeling the familiar rush building inside.

I'm caught by surprise as the energy releases, rushing from me as I hit the place away from the world where nothing exists apart from pure pleasure. The shockwaves pulse outwards, from my body and something nearby crashes to the floor as I cry out. I collapse onto Xander, panting against his ear as the aftershocks run through. With a growl, he roughly turns me over and positions himself behind me, and I gasp out a breath as he slides himself along my sensitive flesh before slamming himself into me.

I could fight back, match his strength, show him I can win, but I understand. This is us, acknowledging we need to meet halfway. Xander wraps my hair around his hand and pulls my head back, and the sharp pain joins the exquisite feeling of him moving inside. My muscles clench around him as he brings me to the edge again; and he swears and makes a guttural noise as he pushes into me one last time.

Glass shatters.

"Fuck, not again," he pants as shards hit him from the broken lightbulb. I suppress a laugh, lost in our moment where our crazy strength bursts around the way it does whenever we fight—demons and ourselves.

His chest is damp against my back as he drops himself onto me, moving hair from my neck to kiss the skin. We lie for a moment, in the silence that joined our frantic sex, before Xander rolls onto one side and hugs me to him.

I don't know what to say. What to think. I lie with my eyes closed coming down from the high and overwhelmed by the intensity of the power that grips us.

"Xander," I whisper. "Talk to me."

His heart thumps against my ear as I lie on his damp chest. "And say what?"

"What you're thinking."

He runs his fingertips across my swollen lips. "You don't want to know."

"I do."

Xander grips me tighter and distracts me with kisses.

He's lying. What Xander means is he doesn't want to say.

So no more words are spoken.

19

Vee

The sound of the door clicking closed rouses me, and I wake in Xander's bed. Alone. A mug and a plate with toast resting on the bedside table. Xander's attempt at showing he cares without having to say something?

We didn't speak much last night, but the way Xander stroked my hair, and ran his gentle touch across my skin, before holding me all night told me more. He can attempt to avoid talking, but he knows as well as I do that it's impossible to avoid the bond between our hearts and souls.

I take the plate and mug downstairs and sit with Seth in the kitchen as the guys discuss their plans in the next room.

Seth's quiet today, and each hour he's with us he becomes quieter and more introspective. Has he accepted anymore of the world now he's experienced it?

"How are you today, Seth?" I wipe toast crumbs from my fingers. "Did you eat?"

He spins his coffee mug on the table in front. "This is real, isn't it? Is this what's behind all the conspiracies? Angels and demons?"

"Angels?" I give a short laugh. "There aren't any angels."

At least I don't think there are angels. Please don't let there be angels, or my mind will explode.

"But there are demons. I've tried to explain everything to myself, but what's in front of my eyes is more believable than any theory I can come up with."

How much can I tell Seth without exploding his mind too? The guys continue their conversation, and I hold one with Seth. He remains silent as I give him a run down on what's happening in my life, but leave out the part about my non-existence. I explain about fae, and Portia, and the struggles between the demons and the Horsemen. As I relay the information, the gaps in my knowledge appear again.

What are the portals and where are they?

Who are they?

Who am I?

However hard I attempt to assimilate to my new life, the last two questions haunt me.

Vee

The guys decide strength in numbers for a visit to the Collector. They're laid back about it, confident they can "extract" the information needed. Who is this guy? If he's more powerful than Portia, I'm unsure what to expect.

I worry about becoming involved with another person the guys normally leave alone, apart from when necessary, and their attempt to keep out of politics. But the world is shifting, and I'm worried what this means for humans too.

The Collector's house is located in a small suburb, set apart from the Victorian terraces, behind a walled garden. The townhouse is three stories high, and holds a presence in the street to match the one I imagine he has. The neatly tended roses add a welcome rainbow of colour to the dreary weather. We stand on the wide polished step and wait as the doorbell tinkles and echoes through the house. Footsteps sound, and a girl opens the door.

She's late teens maybe, dressed in a long, blue, shift dress. Her white blonde hair is braided into a band across her head, and her faraway expression drifts away as she's confronted by the six of us. The fae's violet eyes fill with suspicion.

"We're here to speak to the Collector," Xander says in a gruff tone.

"Do you have an appointment?"

"Yes," replies Heath. "We spoke to him this morning."

Him. The guy has no name. He refuses to go by any other than the Collector. Joss reckons this is to disguise his true identity, but if his magic is powerful why would he need to?

She nods and opens the door. We step into a tiled hallway, the original features intact, from the glass and wrought metal light fittings to the vintage black and white wallpaper covering the walls. The warm house is filled with a mingled floral and spice scent.

"This way." She escorts us to a sitting room, furnished

with a winged and worn burgundy armchair and a matching sofa. Between them, there's a low table adorned with a white cloth and purple candles. I sit on the sofa facing the bay window, as if I'm in a waiting room. The rest of the room is bare save for tall houseplants in pots on the polished wooden floor and smaller potted red flowers in the window.

"Would you like some tea?" the fae girl asks with a bored air. "We only have herbal."

Joss laughs under his breath. "I bet."

"Nope," says Xander. "We don't have time."

She tilts her head and looks down her nose at him. "He may be some time. He has a client."

Ewan checks his watch. "What? We arranged 11:00 a.m."

She pouts a small smile and walks away. Ewan immediately stands and paces around the room, pulling the sheer lilac curtains to one side to look out of the window.

"For someone who collects things, he doesn't have much on display," says Seth.

"I doubt the items he collects are things he wants people to see or touch," replies Ewan.

"How does the place feel to you?" he asks Joss.

Joss rubs his cheek. "Odd, but not dangerous. Vee?"

"I'm not comfortable, but I don't know if that's because of him, or because something's wrong."

"There's a lot of magic around." Xander stands too and walks to the corner, inspecting the plants. "As you'd expect."

"I don't like the place." All eyes turn to Seth. "It feels weird in here, and I've had enough of weird."

"We won't be here long," I say.

"I'm sick of visiting places like this. I've spent three days with my stomach in knots not knowing what'll happen to me next."

"How's your arm?" asks Joss.

"Not too bad, thank you." He touches his injury. "And I would've liked tea."

I suppress a laugh at the expression on Xander's face. "Tea? Seriously?"

"Maybe a glass of water?"

"Dude...," mutters Heath.

"What? They offered." He turns his attention to Xander. "What happened to your cheek?"

Crap. I look into my lap to avoid meeting Xander's eyes. How was I to know my slap would bruise him? Nobody else has mentioned the mark on Xander's face, I'd hoped nobody would.

"Does it matter?" he snaps back.

"Whoa. Okay."

Xander flops into the single armchair. "The Collector had better not take long."

We sit silently for a few minutes and I listen to the loud tick from the vintage clock on the fireplace mantle. Ewan sniffs at his jacket. "I'm gonna walk out of here smelling bloody awful. The smell makes me feel sick."

"A little cloying," says Joss. "I agree."

Ewan shakes his head at him. "Fancy words again."

Joss came with us, despite complaining he'd rather stay at the house, and spent the journey staring out the car window not speaking to anybody. I'm finding it harder to sense how he feels. Is Joss shutting down on me? Now, he has his elbow on the sofa arm, propping up his head, the dark circles beneath his eyes more pronounced.

As soon as I get the chance, I'm talking to him about this. I refuse to let him hide from me what's happening.

The door to the room creaks open and a tall man strides in. He stands in front of Xander and looks down.

"I'd like to take my seat. Please." His voice has a hint of an accent; European, but I can't tell where. France? Spain?

I squeeze my eyes closed. *Please don't get riled, Xander.*

The Collector's blond hair is pulled into a ponytail, the curls springing to below his neck. He's barefoot, in leather pants and a loose shirt woven in rainbow colours. He turns, and when his bright green eyes land on me a sensation similar to the one from Logan washes over. My mind feels invaded, as if long fingers are probing inside.

Xander stands and the Collector breaks his gaze then takes his seat.

"It's been some time since you visited me," he says.

I expected the Collector to have an appearance to match his formal home, but if anything, he looks like a rock star. To many, he probably is. If he's as old as they say, there's no sign of wear to his smooth, luminous skin or in his pale blue eyes.

"We prefer to ignore you and stay away," replies Heath. "But it seems that a few people we usually ignore are coming to our attention."

"Yes. I spoke to Syv. She filled me in on the details." He taps the wooden chair arm with purple painted fingernails. "You really are in a mess, aren't you?"

"We're fine. Just piecing things together."

His mouth twitches at one corner. "I think you're unaware how much chaos surrounds you." He waves a hand at Seth. "Especially him."

Xander sits forward. "His life has been threatened by someone in the supernatural world, and we need to find out who. People are dying."

The Collector's focus remains on Seth who stares back at him. Can Seth feel the same invasion in his mind too? "Interesting."

The room falls silent and Xander shifts next to me, his impatience apparent to us all. The Collector sits back and steeples his fingers beneath his chin.

"And your lives are threatened too?" he asks.

"As always, but you know the outcome from each time we die," says Heath in a low voice.

"Yes. Clever Death's resurrection skills. I've known Horsemen before you," replies the Collector.

The tension in the room explodes into a mixture of emotions from the guys, confusion and fear mingled with curiosity.

"What do you mean?" asks Joss in a sharp tone.

"But never a Fifth." He points at me with a long finger, panic stabbing at my heart as he does. "Are you Verity?"

I nod.

"When did you know them? Who were they?" demands Xander.

He flicks his fingers dismissively. "I don't remember. Like you don't, I suppose. You're always filled with self-importance and bravado, and my being in exile keeps me away from everything but those who want to help me."

"Please tell me he's lying," says Heath below his breath.

Stupefied, I shake my head.

"Come on. I've lived in this world two hundred years. I see you come and go. I'll be interested to see how this plays out."

"What happened to them?" Xander leans forward palms on his knees. "What killed them?"

"Were they killed? I don't know. I think they were just retrieved. Taken off duty, if you like." He flicks his fingers. "But you Horsemen always *feel* the same."

Joss stands. "Taken by who?"

"I don't know, and I don't care." He gestures at Joss to sit again, but he doesn't.

"But you live in this world! Of course you care," protests Heath.

"Like I said, I've been here two hundred years. I don't fear anything." He sighs. "I'll survive. And I'm not here to talk about your history. I can spare you ten minutes. What is it you wanted to know?"

Xander pauses long enough to receive an arched brow from the Collector. He stands and straightens his shirtsleeves. "Oh, well, if there's nothing to talk about, I'll leave you. I'm a busy man."

"No. We have questions. Did Syv tell you what happened to Taron?" asks Ewan.

"Yes. Sad state of affairs, but again of no interest to me."

"He was killed with magic, we think caused by a rune we haven't seen before. Syv thinks it's ancient fae magic." Xander pulls out his phone and passes it to the Collector. "If you could help confirm this, at least we know we're looking for fae and not demons."

Seth drops his head back on the sofa and stares at the ceiling. Any mention of supernatural races, and he zones out.

The Collector traces the shape with a finger, brow tugged together. "What did this do to Taron?"

"Killed him."

"I mean, how did he die?"

"It affected his memory, and then consumed him from inside. He was drowning in his own blood. Painfully and horrifically." Joss squeezes my hand. "We ended his life rather than let him die slowly."

The Collector rises. "I do recognise this, but not without

checking exactly what it means. I require a book from my study."

"Joss, go with him," says Xander. "We'll wait here."

I stand. "I'd like to go too."

"Safety in numbers?" says the Collector with a light laugh. "Perhaps Dina could bring the rest of you you some tea now?"

20

Vee

"Do you have a real name?" I blurt as the Collector leads us along the wooden hallway towards a wide set of stairs.

He pauses and smiles at me. "I did, but I don't use it anymore. It's not relevant to this world."

We tramp up the carpeted stairs, behind him, passed closed doors with ornate gold handles, until we reach a locked door. The Collector pulls a silver chain around his neck from beneath his shirt revealing a small key.

I imagine all studies to be like Joss's, compact and claustrophobic, filled with a musty-book scent. This one is as big as my whole flat was. Books span the wall, floor to ceiling, co-ordinated by their leather-bound colour. The largest are stacked out of reach, smaller ones at knee height.

Besides the shelves, the room contains period furniture to match the overall feel of the house: a large desk with high-backed chair and a large cabinet with glass doors at the far end of the room.

Joss stands, hands in pockets, and watches as the Collector rests against a large desk and flicks his fingers. A spiralling white energy drifts from the tips across the room before darting upwards. The magic flares as it hits a book that flies into the Collector's outstretched hand.

"Is the answer in there?" asks Joss.

"I suspect so." The Collector turns and opens the large book, placing a slender hand on the pages to prevent the book closing. He closes his eyes and a faint ultraviolet light surrounds his finger, leaving an imprint when he pulls it away.

"Pass me the phone so I can examine the rune." He holds his hand out and Joss passes it to him. He places the phone on the table and flicks through the book, eyes darting between the screen and pages covered in symbols and letters that don't form words I know.

The longer the Collector flicks through, the faster he moves, and he hunches over, swearing as he reaches the last few pages.

"I can't find it, but that symbol is definitely from a school of magic not practiced any more."

"Not even by you?" asks Joss.

"No." He crosses to another shelf and crouches, before pulling a book out. The tiny book is half the size of the note pads Ewan writes on. The paper inside is thick, the scratchy writing in black ink. The Collector leafs through to the back and compares a symbol on the page to the image on Xander's phone screen.

"Where's the book from?" asks Joss.

"I don't remember. I like collecting books." He gestures at the wall to ceiling shelves crammed to overflowing, and the pile on his table, then to the cabinet across the room. "Amongst other things."

"Can I look?" I ask.

His face brightens. "Of course, I'm very proud of my collection."

The "proud collection" is set neatly inside, grouped into varieties of artefact. Some are small figures crafted from clay or china; others are carved bone or wood. Ornate jewellery set with gleaming blue and red gems draws my eye, and a shiver trips along my spine. Is anything here dangerous?

"I'm always looking for powerful items; I like to keep them out of others' hands." He sighs. "Humans put items in museums if they find them, which is dangerous. Anybody could take them, although most have no idea what any of these do."

"And I don't suppose you're going to tell us, are you?" asks Joss.

He smiles broadly. "Correct." He waves the small book. "Let's return to your friends so we can talk about this."

XANDER

Sitting between Ewan and Seth, I watch with scorn as Seth drinks the herbal tea the fae chick brought him. While Joss and Vee are with the Collector, I itch to leave the room and snoop around the guy's house. But we're running out of options and pissing the Collector off won't help.

His admission he knew other Horsemen before freaks

me out. I avoid thinking about what happened to our predecessors, confident we can't die. On days the questions enter my head, I push them away before answers I don't like appear in my mind. But what happens? Did past Horsemen fail to keep portals closed and find themselves stuck on the other side? Is there somebody out there who's strong enough to kill us, and that's why Horsemen need replacing?

I freeze the thoughts out.

The dreams we share are enough to deal with. Are they hints at what I was? Or where I was? The visions come in snapshots, never clear enough to see, but the voices and sounds around hit a familiarity inside that I can't explain.

Two places alternate in mine: one filled with men shouting and crying in agony. The other: me, doing the same.

I'm worried that one day the veil will lift, and I'll see what's happening and where I am.

I'm terrified I'll see blood on my hands.

"Are you okay?"

I blink back to reality, surprised by Seth's concern. "Yeah. Impatient. As usual."

Seth gives a wry smile. "I want answers as much as you do. I always knew something was wrong with the world. But this..."

Seth. I want to trust him. I need to trust him, and he's cooperated with everything so far. Am I too harsh, unable to see past my suspicion to his attack and the death sentence over his head? But there's something weird about him I can't place my finger on. He's too quiet. I don't know what's really going on with him.

I sure as hell want that laptop back from Seth and him kept off the internet in case he leads anybody to us.

The door opens, and the Collector reappears with Joss

and Vee. They remain standing in the doorway. I'm happy to see Joss more animated; he's been odd recently. Is Vee putting pressure on him that he doesn't want? Something isn't right, and I need to talk to him later. Normally, I would've quizzed him, especially after the incident at the storage place, but everything has been non-stop crazy. At least nothing hurt him when we were there.

"Well?" I ask. "What did you discover?"

The Collector crosses to sit in his chair and holds up a small book. "Your rune is in here."

I sit upright. "What does it mean? Can you help us find whoever cast it?"

"This isn't fae, or demon, or even witch. This predates us all... Whoever used this rune on Taron is more powerful than any entity I'm aware of." He flicks through the pages. "I can't read every word in this language so I have no clear idea how to cast this spell, I'm afraid, but I can understand enough to know basically how it works.

"How?" I ask.

The Collector places the book down. "The spell works like a time bomb. The magic from the rune spreads like wires through the victim's body, ready to detonate and is painless until activated. The text explains a predetermined action will trigger it, as if setting something to self-destruct."

"So Taron was a weapon?" asks Heath.

"Or somebody wanted him dead after he fulfilled his role." The Collector snaps the book closed. "What happened to trigger the spell?"

"We were questioning Taron about who employed him."

"And the spell stopped him answering. That was the trigger."

Joss reaches out for the book but the Collector moves it

out of his reach. "What energy does the rune use to focus the magic? If you can't, who could? Demons?"

"No. I told you, this is primordial. Whoever created this book existed before any of us." He pushes the book closed. "And whoever did this to Taron has access to magic thought to be trapped in other realms."

Joss takes a sharp breath. "Are you saying someone passed through a portal into this world recently?"

"Or has been well hidden for some time." He steals a glance at Vee, and his mouth curves into a smile. "As you were, Verity."

"I don't know magic!" she protests. "And I certainly didn't attack my friend."

"I was not implying such a thing." He turns to Seth. "Why does somebody want to kill you?"

"Because of my hobby." I frown at his strange answer.

"Is that so? A dangerous one it seems." He turns his attention back to me. "As the humans like to say, you have your work cut out."

Ewan sits forward. "We bloody know that. What we want is to know if you can help us?"

"If you can find a cipher to translate the full text or name the runes, you'll be a step closer to pinpointing how far back this magic goes. I'm afraid I don't know where to find anything connected to this. I focus on collecting fae items."

"Could Syv find it?" asks Vee.

"Possibly." He laces his fingers together on his lap. "She has some interesting skills and usually locates items quickly. The problem is, you don't know what you're looking for."

"For fuck's sake," mutters Heath. "Here we go again."

Seth clears his throat. "May I look at the book, please?"

The Collectors mouth curves into amusement at his overpoliteness. "Why? Do you speak an ancient language?"

"No. But I have come across people sharing symbols recently." He glances at Ewan. "On the message boards."

"Why didn't you say?" snaps Ewan. "I never saw them!"

"You didn't ask. All you asked for was Nova Pharm info."

Ewan's face darkens, but he doesn't respond.

The Collector leans forward and passes the small book to Seth, who opens it and leafs through as if the pages might tear. Seth pauses on some pages, and flicks back and forth, pushing his glasses up where they slide along his nose.

His mouth parts and cheeks redden as he points at a page with a shaking finger. "This one. I've seen this one."

Resisting temptation to snatch the book off him, I peer over his shoulder. A symbol very different to the one we saw marked on Taron is written on the page with the archaic language beneath. This one is a series of lines that create a sideways triangle with interconnected squares arranged inside.

"Somebody pass me their phone." Seth holds out a palm. "Quick. Let me show you this."

I've never seen the guy this animated; and the room falls silent as Seth locates something online. Smiling in triumph, he shoves the phone at me. "Look at this site for a new charity foundation. It's linked to Nova Pharm because one of the board members founded it. We're not sure of the link between the two yet. That's one thing we were getting close to when figuring out all their hidden projects."

The symbol onscreen is the same as on his page. Hidden in the centre of the logo representing the Myriad Foundation black against the blue, is a runic message to anybody who recognises the magic.

I break into a smile to match Seth's. "Fuck, yeah." Taking back the phone, I then pass it to Ewan. Each of us studies the symbol; Ewan brightens and Vee smiles, but Joss blinks and passes it to Heath with no response.

What the hell is with him?

Heath stands and waves the phone. "Take some photos of what's in the book and we get onto this. Xander?"

For the first time in days, the fog clears and a new optimism steps forward.

A connection.

A direction.

We're going to end this.

21

Vee

A buoyant Xander lifts everybody else's mood, and he leaves the Collector's house with renewed determination. Seth finally agrees to move more items from his place to the guys' house, and Xander and Heath leave with him in Heath's car.

But not before dark mutterings about "trusting the bastard" from a pissed off Ewan, easily heard by us all. Joss is keen to get home, and I'd rather spend time resting, so the three of us head back to the house in Joss's car.

Joss heads straight upstairs when we arrive, without a word. His behaviour worries me, but he refuses to talk.

Tired and hungry, I head to find something to eat. I'll check on him later.

With Joss upstairs, and the other three guys out, I finally find time alone with Ewan. Or I could if he'd detach himself from his laptop for ten minutes.

I walk up behind him and wrap my arms around his neck. Placing my head on Ewan's shoulder, I inhale the woody scent of his cologne, evoking memories of last time we were alone at this kitchen table.

On this kitchen table.

"Take a break, Ewan. I want to talk to you."

He shrugs me away as I nip his earlobe. "I'm busy."

Wow. Okay. "You're at Xander level on the grumpy scale today. What's wrong?"

"This shit worries me." He gestures at his laptop. "Seth told me where to find the info on the charity foundation, and I'm digging around their site and connections to find any fae or demon links to it."

I sit beside him. "Have you found anything?"

Ewan nods. "The board member's name is Alasdair Faulkner. He's been on the Nova Pharm board for a couple of years, and the charity foundation was set up several months ago. I can't 100% figure out what the charity does. Something community based. They have a launch coming up soon and will reveal everything then, apparently."

"Hmm. We need to look into attending that."

"Yeah. I've also found some evidence of payments from Nova Pharm to the Myriad Foundation, but they're trying to keep the connection secret. I can't figure out why."

"And is he human?"

"I'm unsure. I think so, I can't find links to anybody on our watch list and his human background looks legit."

"Well, if there's a magic symbol on the foundation's logo, somebody is using it as a front, whether the guy is human or not."

"Yeah. So we need to talk to Syv too and ask if she's been sent to find anything that could link to this type of magic."

"Do you think she has?"

Ewan chews his bottom lip. "She might have an assignment to look for something already. I hope she does because then we can discover what we need."

"So we have the next items on Xander's 'to do' list?" I smile but Ewan doesn't. "He'll be happy you confirmed what Seth thought."

"Yeah." He taps a pen on the table. "Xander can come up with the finer details. We'll figure out a way to get closer to the guy running the foundation, and I expect he'll line up another meeting with Syv too."

Why doesn't Ewan sound happier we've found a way forward and some solid leads? I close the lid to his laptop, keeping my hand on the top. Ewan frowns at me. He's sullen, the old Ewan from early days. What did I do?

"Can I ask you something? Why did you tell Xander about the night at the Warehouse?"

"I didn't. I don't know who told him," he says gruffly.

I straighten. "Do all four of you know now?"

"Yep. I'd apologise to you, but I didn't tell them."

"Xander wasn't happy with me, and we argued. Whoever told him put trouble between us we could've avoided."

Ewan sighs. "Yeah, he certainly let me know that too. Heath wasn't much happier."

"And Joss?"

"He didn't comment. Ask him yourself." He pushes my hand away and flips the laptop lid back open.

Whoa. I push it closed again. "Ewan. What's wrong with you?" Is this about Xander? Does he know? I always worried one guy might be jealous, or not cope with the idea I sleep with them all, but never Ewan.

"Do you want to go out somewhere, sometime?" he asks.

"Now you're confusing me. You're behaving like you're

pissed off with me, now you're asking me out on a date? Are you asking me out?"

He taps the laptop lid. "I thought maybe we could do some ordinary shit. A meal. Movies. I dunno, whatever people do when they're not trying to prevent an apocalypse."

There's a hint of a smile, but this isn't him. He avoids the real world. "What is this attitude really about?"

Ewan runs both hands down his face and leans back in his chair. "I thought it might help if you spent time around people, not just us. I'm worried about you, Vee. We all stay connected to our human side, but you're determined to be rid of it. Why?"

My stomach flips over. "Has Joss spoken to you?"

"Yes. Vee, imagine what the five of us would be like, if we all let go of our humanity. Don't you think our ability to connect to humans is what makes us who we are? Without that, we're no better than any of the creatures we fight."

"Maybe you'll find we're stronger if we're more distant from humans, especially if something worse than you've faced before is coming. I don't mean that I want to lose my humanity, Ewan. I just can't cope with human emotions. I refuse to be the girl falling apart because she's freaked out by death. I'm a Horseman. I'm one of you, and I need those weaker emotions gone."

"Wow. I can't believe this is you talking. You're not the girl I first met, not anymore."

"That's the whole point. I'm not, and I never will be. Not since that moment I killed the incubus. You know that."

He shakes his head and turns back to his laptop. I stare at the side of his head, at the messy hair dipping into his eyes and his pursed lips. Anger rises at him ignoring me.

I shove my chair back and stand. "Why are you being so bloody rude?"

No response. If I stay here, this building anger could lead to words I don't want to say. The suddenness of the reaction surprises me, as if I'm gripped by more than the annoyance he's not affectionate tonight.

Deep inside, buried in the centre of who I am, is a need for Ewan. I have to connect with him; he can't hold back.

This is pointless. As I leave, I hear his chair scrape too and pause at the kitchen door.

"I don't know what to say to you. You're not listening to me."

He approaches and closes the door, resting his hand against the wood so I can't leave. "You want to be a killing machine and nothing else? You want sex to be about satisfaction and not love? That's what emotionless means."

I blink at his words. "No."

"A hard heart won't have room for us, Vee."

The hidden Ewan revealed himself over the last few minutes, the one keeping his distance but worrying about me more deeply than the others. They must all have discussed my thoughts and situation, but none had words like Ewan's tonight.

In his eyes, I see the same as the last time we hid away with each other. Ewan shares his deepest feelings through the unhidden deep affection in them, and for the first time, I realise what my desire to lose my emotions means.

I might lose the ability to love them. Is that the darkness? The part inside my soul that wants those emotions gone because they're inconvenient. Who is she? Ewan's right, that Vee isn't who I am.

"You don't trust me, do you?" I ask.

"Of course I do."

"Then why are you holding back from me? I thought we were getting closer and then 'bam' barriers up. You don't touch me anymore."

"Because I'm not sure it's a good idea for us to take this further."

"Because you think I'll hurt you? That I'll drain your powers if we have sex?"

"That's not why, Vee." He places a hand on my face. The other guys are tall and muscular, but Ewan's heavyset build extends to the hand that all but encompasses one side of my face. "I'm worried about what might happen."

His touch rushes through me, my desire for him surging. "About what?"

"I'm the last, aren't I?" He withdraws his hand and shoves both into his jeans pockets. "I don't know what will happen once you've had sex with all of us."

What the hell is he saying? "Nothing will happen apart from I'll have the closeness to you all that I want, Ewan. I want to be with the Ewan who opened up to me, who made me feel the way I did."

He stares at his feet. "But you want to let go of the Vee who made *me* feel the way I did. She's who I want to connect with, and I already feel her retreating. "

"That's not true."

"My powers, Vee. I know when you have sex with the others something between you joins and intensifies their powers. Xander's strength, Joss's empathy, and Heath's ability to give life." He looks back up, eyes glittering. "What do I offer the world? Disease. Do you think I want my expression of how I feel about you to create pain? Can you imagine how horrific that idea is?"

"That wouldn't happen, I'm sure. Maybe there's more inside that you haven't discovered yet and that will trigger?

You hang back when you fight, and don't use your powers much. Why?"

He fixes me with an unwavering look. "Because I hate them."

Heath complains about his role, but accepts his powers. They all struggle to an extent, but I've never seen any look as lost as Ewan right now. "Ewan..."

"Don't look at me like that." Ewan takes my shirt collar and pulls me towards him, his mouth close to mine. The desire immediately dizzies, the need to kiss him pushing away our conversation from my mind. Ewan slides his hand into my hair, thumb circling the nape and sending a shiver through.

"I care about you on a level I don't want to. I love Vee, the girl who walked into our lives and surprised the hell out of me." He digs his hand deeper into my hair. "In the beginning, I swore whoever this Truth girl is, she wouldn't affect me, but you walked into the pub that day with Heath and tore away that resolve. Now, the girl who teased my feelings out of me, who took away my self-control because I wanted her so badly, wants to lose herself. And I'm scared I'll be the one to make that happen."

I brush my mouth against his, his stubble scraping against my cheek. "You won't."

He places his thumb to my jaw and steadies my face with his large hand. He inhales sharply before he responds with the kiss I've ached for. Ewan kisses me deeper and harder than before, the type of kiss that turns the world into a dream and snatches away thoughts of anything but being in this moment with him.

Lacing my fingers into his hair, I hold Ewan's face to mine, wanting to kiss away the worry holding him back. He can't push me away, not this time.

Ewan breaks the kiss, then touches my lips and looks at me with pure, plain desire. "What if who I am destroys the human inside you?"

Is this why I react with this new intensity to cross the line with Ewan? Because something within me needs him to fulfill who I am? And now he knows what I asked of Joss, is this why he avoids me?

"But the human was to disguise me. You all have to accept she'll go, but I'll be stronger."

"And that's the problem," he whispers. "We don't know what that means. The Vee I met would never want to lose part of who she is.

The desire and anger mingle with my need to have the guys do what I ask. "I'm still the Vee you met. I might not be the vulnerable girl from the night you saved me, but I still hold you in my heart. That won't change." I push my lips against Ewan's, holding his face to mine. The hesitation isn't there as he roughly kisses me back, wrapping his arms around my waist and holding me close. However gentle Ewan can be, the strength in the muscles surrounding me isn't.

I hold him tight, refusing to take my mouth from his, as if he's the air I need to breathe, desperate and yielding. I dizzy to a new high as his tongue explores my mouth and his taste intoxicates me further.

But Ewan pulls away. My heart twists in pain as he holds me at arms' length, hands gripping my shoulders. I'm on the verge of launching myself at him, at showing him how strong I am, and convincing him this is what we need to do, but one thing stops me. His expression. I don't want Ewan to look at me with this wariness; I don't want us to only be driven by my need to unite our powers.

I want Ewan to look at me with eyes filled with passion

and love, not this shut-down guy whose response would only be primal lust. I want this to be about us, about showing him I'm Vee and giving ourselves to each other.

I've fooled myself that Xander is the one who resists me; I broke through his barriers much quicker than Ewan's.

"You're the heart of us all, Vee. Don't destroy who we are."

His heart races beneath my palm when I rest it on his shirt, as it betrays the feelings he unleashed. We stand, locked in a moment a world away from the last time we were here. A moment where I know I'll need to fight harder for Ewan than anyone else.

"I need time out." Ewan grabs his leather jacket from the chair. I watch in shock, as the thread linking my heart to his pulls tight, then snaps as he walks out of the door without saying goodbye.

I slump onto a kitchen chair and hold my head in my hands, hair falling forward to brush the table. Ewan's bike rumbles to life, and the roar distances as he drives away, echoing through the day. My cheek smarts from our kisses, his taste on my lips, and I fight the welling tears. My head's a mess. A complete fucking mess.

I thought I knew who I was, and what I needed, but I don't at all. If I lose my emotions, I will also lose who I am to them. Ewan's words and behaviour made this clear. In my heart, I know I want to keep the ability to love and care. So why is there another Vee inside demanding I sacrifice this to become who I need to be?

Will she consume me?

22

Joss

The sense something follows me grows as the hours pass. Sometimes I catch a glimpse in the corner of my eye, a shadow moving, but when I blink or look around there's nothing in the room. This could be my tired eyesight, but I'm terrified something will overcome me again.

I don't want to go to that place a second time.

Worse, each time I remember, the fear grows and my mind fogs. Now when the gripping anxiety leaves, I feel less. A lack of anything. Even around Vee, I don't have the same desire for her. It's as if I'm still trapped in the cage, suffocating.

Ewan and I spoke to Xander and Heath about what happened, and I mentioned to Vee how I'm exhausted and about the encounter I don't understand. When I downplayed how I'm feeling, she seemed confident I'd be okay.

I wish I was.

Our visit to the Collector barely registers with me. We went, retrieved information, and left. Usually I'd question someone a lot more than I did, but I didn't care. Couldn't be bothered. All I want to do is sleep; an exhaustion I haven't felt before. I don't care. I'm tired and just want a break from this shit. I told Vee and Ewan I wanted to lie down, and that's exactly my intention.

I prop my hands above my head and stare at the lampshade above, fighting the drowsiness. The shadows intensify each time I doze off, as does my fear the vision will return with them.

But I'm so fucking tired. My eyelids flutter as I attempt to stay awake. In my semi-conscious state, I dream the shadow grows and drifts around my room. As I'm dragged deeper into unconsciousness, the darkness grows.

The shadow is here and morphs into a tall figure, and the last of my energy drains away.

Vee

I wander from the kitchen towards the lounge room, confusion following me. What do I do now? My intention to lie on the sofa and lick my wounds dissipates as I reach the bottom of the stairs.

I can't pass.

A dread grips, washing over me, and paralyses every muscle. Demon? No, but something is wrong, a discomfort running through I haven't felt since the day Ewan was attacked. My heart races and breathing shortens as if I'm about to have a panic attack, and I have to fight the instinct to run from the house. I stare at the steps leading upstairs in front of me.

Joss is up there.

I curl my hand around the stair rail and focus on breathing and channelling out the fear, forcing my power through to squeeze the dread away. What the hell is happening? I slump to the bottom step and struggle to stand again.

Joss.

Pushing away the paralysis as concern for him overtakes the fear for myself, I run up the stairs, two at a time. Joss's bedroom door is shut, and his room silent. Whatever presence is causing my weird reaction grows as the dread shivers further through me, dragging the paralysis down my spine again. I reach out, but the door handle won't move. Stepping back, I summon the strength from the War fighting through and smack my shoulder into the hard wood.

The door slams open, hitting Joss's bedroom wall with a crash.

An incorporeal dark figure sits on Joss's chest, what look like hands covering his face. Joss doesn't struggle, or move, and the figure grows in size before my eyes, stretching upwards towards the ceiling, a swirling black mass darkening the room. An intense cold adds more chill to my blood and the dread feeling intensifies.

I'm too stunned to move or speak, unable to form a plan what to do. At the noise, the apparition shifts away from Joss and toward me; the edges mist into an arm shape and reach out.

Red eyes glow somewhere in the centre, but the spectre swirls in and out of shape. There's no face. No expression. No clue where I should attack.

The shape rushes at me before I can summon any power: I don't know what would work. Where would I hit it if I took on War? Where's its heart to target with Death's magic? How can I turn this incorporeal presence into dust using Famine? The options fly through my head, and I'm lost.

I brace myself for an assault, prepared for whatever power will take hold. Instead, the darkness flies by my head and through the bedroom door and my face smarts as if an Arctic wind has hit me.

I whirl around, but there's nothing in the hallway. Should I hunt whatever it is? But what's the point when I have no clue how to kill whatever it is? I cautiously approach Joss's prone figure. His skin has a jaundiced yellow hue, eyes sunken into his sockets and surrounded by dark circles. I place a hand on his forehead, panic returning as I look at his blue lips and the sharp collarbones digging against his shirt and replacing the lean muscle.

"Joss?" My voice is edged with panic, hoarse and tiny in the middle of the horror.

He's cold. Unmoving.

I take his wrist, but already know the answer. I can't sense anything from him—no fear, no pain, only emptiness. This tells me exactly what Joss's non-existent pulse confirms.

Whatever was in the room with us killed him.

And Heath isn't here.

To be continued in The Four Horsemen: Chaos

Books by Lisa Swallow

Like contemporary romance? I write those too!
What would you prefer to read?

British rock star romance?
Try broody Dylan...
Summer Sky

Or bad boy Jax...
Cadence

College romance at an English university?
Because of Lucy

Hollywood romance?
Unscripted

A gamer romance?
End Game

And More....
amazon.com/author/lisaswallow

Acknowledgments

A special thanks to those who continue to support me in this crazy writing world!

A special thanks to Lou for her support, friendship and for your honesty and help.

Thanks also to Chelle Whitaker for her pre-ARC read and advice. I promise I'll destroy the room next time.

Thanks also to all the lovely readers who are members of the Four Horsemen readers group and share my excitement for the series. And a thank you to my ARC team for spotting errors.

Thank you to Krys Janae from TakeCover Designs for the beautiful cover art, and to Peggy for her editing excellence and friendship.

And thank you all for taking a chance on The Four Horsemen and reading the series!

ABOUT THE AUTHOR

LJ Swallow is a USA Today bestselling paranormal romance and urban fantasy author who is the alter-ego of USA Today bestselling contemporary romance author Lisa Swallow.

Giving in to her dark side, LJ spends time creating worlds filled with supernatural creatures who don't fit the norm, and heroines who are more likely to kick ass than sit on theirs.

For more information:
ljswallow.com
lisa@lisaswallow.net

Printed in Great Britain
by Amazon